a road with no end

To Judy,

    With warmest regards,

        Mochtar Lubis

        Jakarta, 5 August '80

MOCHTAR LUBIS

a road with no end

Translated from the Indonesian and edited
by Anthony H. Johns

 HUTCHINSON OF LONDON

HUTCHINSON & CO (*Publishers*) LTD
178–202 Great Portland Street, London W1

London Melbourne Sydney
Auckland Bombay Toronto
Johannesburg New York

First published in Indonesian under the title
Djalan tak ada Udjung in 1952

*This book has been set in Baskerville, printed in Great Britain
on Antique Wove paper by Balding & Mansell Ltd.,
Wisbech and London, and bound by Wm. Brendon & Son Ltd.,
of Tiptree, Essex.*
09 089420 0

To Hally and my children

Contents

Introduction	*page*	1
Chapter 1		17
Chapter 2		35
Chapter 3		47
Chapter 4		61
Chapter 5		69
Chapter 6		89
Chapter 7		117
Chapter 8		122
Chapter 9		132
Chapter 10		137

Introduction

Mochtar Lubis is one of the best-known of Indonesian journalists, and an outstanding personality by any criteria. He was born in 1920 in the Minangkabau region of central Sumatra, his parents belonging to a clan of the north Sumatran Bataks, a group celebrated for their sturdy independence of spirit and forthright manner. After the normal six years of schooling from the age of seven to thirteen, he spent three years at a business college, but for the rest is self-educated, and to a quite remarkable level.

As early as 1945 he had made his mark in the world of Indonesian journalism, and was fully committed to the cause of the Republic, with a courage both moral and physical. A story is told that, after Dutch troops began to return to Indonesia late in that year, a group of pro-Dutch Ambonese soldiers, offended by the consistent nationalism of his articles, forced their way into his office to beat him up. They found that Lubis—a sturdy six-footer—was more than a match for them, and sent them sprawling out of the door.

His travels have been wide. In the decade before his arrest he had opportunities to visit Malaya, Burma, India, Thailand, Hong Kong, the Philippines, the United States, Japan, Korea, and Australia. Thus he is something of a cosmopolitan, and his knowledge of languages—fluent English, Dutch, French, Spanish, German and Japanese—is equally extensive. As a journalist his energy is matched only by the diversity of his interests, and at one time he was editor of a daily newspaper, as well as a monthly periodical, and was also publisher of a weekly and an associate of the cultural supplement of the quality weekly *Scrutiny* (*Siasat*). However, until his first term of house arrest in 1956, he was best known as the editor of the Djakarta daily *Indonesia Raya*, a paper unsparing in its attacks on corruption in public life. His biggest scoop in this period was the exposure of Sukarno's secret marriage to a second wife, Hartini, in 1950. This resulted in anti-Sukarno protests and demonstrations, particularly from women's organisations, all over Indonesia, and earned him Sukarno's undying hatred.

Yet, although it is as a journalist that he has won a wide public overseas, Lubis has always been more than a journalist. His interests are not merely political in the narrow sense of the word—his principal concern is with Man as man, and human dignity. This is reflected in the breadth of his literary interests in Indonesia and abroad, his involvement in cultural associations, and his own creative writing and numerous translations.

The literary form in which he has been most prolific

is that of the short story, his best being very good indeed. They have their roots in keen observation and a sense of form, so that their devastating satiric bite goes beyond the Indonesian situation to offer a valid comment on human pusillanimity and folly in general. He writes in the tradition of Swift—hard, incisive, belligerently honest, and merciless in the exposure of corruption and humbug. The same journalistic talents were used to striking effect in the first of his books to appear in English—*Twilight in Djakarta*—written while he was in prison, smuggled out of Indonesia in manuscript form, and published in the United Kingdom by Hutchinson in 1963, and the next year in the United States by Vanguard.

Written with verve, it will not quickly lose the topical appeal it had at the time of publication. A fascinating piece of reportage, it gives a graphic picture of the corruption and despair pervading the various levels in Djakartan society during the last years of liberal democracy in Indonesian politics. Here he fought again the battles of 1954–55 when he was still editing *Indonesia Raya*, and used the book to diagnose and illustrate the evil infecting his country's public life, and to highlight the impotence of reason and debate to combat the growing menace to personal truth and human dignity.

However, important thought *Twilight in Djakarta* is, the place of Lubis in modern Indonesian literature had already been established eleven years earlier with the publication of *A Road with No End* (*Djalan tak ada Udjung*) in 1952.

The story of the development of this literature is almost an epic in its own right. Bahasa Indonesia, the Indonesian national language and essentially a modern

3

projection of Malay, was not born as a concept until 1928, despite the thousand years or so of the recorded history of Malay. During the thirties its use as a literary language grew rapidly, but it was the Japanese occupation of 1942 which marked the debut of the Indonesian writer into the essential concerns of modern man. At a stroke the whole fabric of Dutch East Indian Society was destroyed, and one of the side effects of the pillaging of houses and libraries of the Dutch was the release into general circulation of a whole new world of literature and ideas. The small group of Indonesian writers and intelligentsia were thrown back on their own resources, convention and pretence stripped away as everything around them failed them, and they were left with nothing but their naked humanity.

From the shock of this encounter emerged a new group of writers, some of whom were later to be known as the 'Generation of 45'. Their dominating concerns, in their own words, were 'Universal Humanism' and 'Human Dignity', and their leading figure was the symbolist poet Charil Anwar. In February 1950 they published a moving Confession of Faith:

'We are the legitimate heirs of the culture of the whole world, a culture which is ours to extend and develop in our own way. We are born of the common people; and for us, this term implies the inchoate mass from which new and healthy worlds of thought and expression may be born.

'It is not so much our brown skin, black hair and slanting cheek bones that make us Indonesian, but rather what is manifest through our character and way of thinking.

'We do not wish to limit by a name this Indonesian

4

culture of ours. On the other hand we do not understand it as the refurbishing of something old to be a source of self-satisfaction: we envisage it as something vigorous and new. For this Indonesian culture will be determined by the manifold responses made on our part to stimuli from every corner of the globe, each of them true to its own nature. And we will oppose any attempt to restrict or impede a re-examination of our scale of values.

'For us, our revolution implies the discarding of old and outmoded values, fit only for obloquy, and their replacement by new ones. Until this is done our revolution is not complete. Our results may not always be original, but our fundamental quest is humanity, and in our study, analyses and quality of vision we have our own characteristics: further, our attitude to the community in which we live is that of men who are aware of the mutual interaction between artist and society.'

This nobility of utterance, this conscious rejection of chauvinism which characterised the first years of the revolution, was an inspiration to many foreign scholars in quite diverse fields who 'discovered' Indonesia in the years immediately after 1945, and it constitutes the tradition to which Lubis belongs.

Unfortunately, it was a tradition which by 1955 had spent its force. The increasingly rapid economic run-down of the country, disappointed expectations, and the almost totally destructive emotionalism associated with the claim for West New Guinea, then increasing in momentum, was rendering Universal Humanism irrelevant. New foci of interest were asserting themselves at the expense of the older tradition. Socialist Realism, Art for Society, Literature for the Masses, and axioms

5

such as 'Art is as much a tool as an adze or a spanner' gained currency. As the decade progressed, xenophobic nationalism and the Communist Party joined forces in an attempt to drive literature with concerns more human than political to the wall. In 1963 even the poetry of Charil Anwar was condemned on grounds of his existentialist morality and cosmopolitan a-political outlook. In face of all these pressures many writers found creative work impossible and others, with varying degrees of sincerity, espoused the new values and wrote to serve a political cause.

Lubis was one of those who kept faith. He turned away from literature it is true, but he fought against what he saw as a poison infecting the Indonesian scale of values with all his might. He was imprisoned for a month in 1956–7, then kept under house arrest until April 1961, when he took advantage of his release to attend the 10th General Assembly of the International Press Institute in Tel Aviv. Although warned while abroad that he would face a further term of jail if he returned to Indonesia, especially as he had made trenchant criticisms of restrictions on the Press of his homeland in addressing the Assembly, he felt it his duty to return. He was immediately re-arrested and held in detention until Sukarno's fall in 1966, when he emerged with his integrity and enthusiasm intact. Asked how he had endured the years of imprisonment and yet retained his poise, he replied that he had a secret weapon—his wife, Hally. She had given him her unswerving moral support, and had frequently made the long journey to Madiun, where he was held, to take him food, give him news of their two children, and tell him something of the outside world. He had also, in those early years of the

6

revolution, seen a vision, espoused an ideal, and it is this vision and this ideal, and the source of his strength to sustain them, which are enshrined in *A Road with No End*.

The story is set between the re-occupation of Indonesia by the Dutch in 1946 under the aegis of the British and the Dutch violation of the Linggadjati agreement (creating the 'United States of Indonesia' and a 'Netherlands-Indonesian Union'), known as the First Police Action. The central figure is Isa, a school teacher, a mild unassuming man who has suffered the hardships of the Japanese occupation and is now baffled by the confusion and unsettlement of the British interregnum as the Dutch struggle to regain control of their former colony. Isa is not sure where his responsibilities lie, and for a while is uncertain where to turn. In contrast is the spirited revolutionary Hazil, who can speak of his ideals with fluency and conviction, whose watchword is loyalty. The apparently ill-assorted pair are brought together by music. The violin has been a popular instrument in Indonesia since the period of Portuguese cultural and political influence in the archipelago in the sixteenth century, and, besides their shared choice of the same instrument, Hazil is a composer.

Between them is Isa's wife Fatima. Since the first six months of his marriage, Isa has been impotent, and as the unlikely friendship of the two men develops, Hazil is brought closer to Fatima. His betrayal of his friend, by misconduct with her, in a way foreshadows his later and final betrayal of Isa because he cannot endure the Dutch torture.

Isa is a man beset by fear, fear of violence, fear of his wife, fear of the displeasure even of his little adopted

7

son. He is afraid to take any action, utter any word against those around him. This fear is related to the psychological condition which renders him impotent, and which, his doctor says, can only be cured by something outside of and greater than himself. Thus he does not join the revolution out of a sense of patriotism, but, because of his fear of making decisions, events make his decisions for him. He does not choose the revolution, the revolution chooses him. And this 'non-decision' sets him at the beginning of a road with no end—not leading to heroic deeds to be sung in his country's annals, but to a coming to terms with himself, a learning to live with fear, his besetting weakness.

More even than this. Since fear is at the root of his impotence, the road also represents his psychological journey to the recovery of his virility. In this Isa is not just Isa the man, but a symbol of Indonesia, unable to mobilise its energies, unable to activate the social and moral strength of the thousands of meek, little folk such as himself to build a society dedicated to the growth in moral stature of its people and the pursuit of human happiness.

The motif of the road recurs throughout the novel from the first page, when the wheels of a truck drum through the empty streets, following their own twisting road with no end. It fascinates Isa's imagination and haunts his dreams in terrible nightmares, a road on which there is no turning back. Sometimes he sees it revealed for a split second in a flash of lightning piercing total darkness, just as in Djakarta when drizzle brings down the night to the accompaniment of rolls of thunder. There is an echo, too, of the well-known passage from the Kur'an comparing life with a journey through a thunderstorm on a dark night: 'The lightning well nigh snatches away their sight; whensoever it gives them light, they walk in it, and when the darkness is over them, they halt' (Kur'an 2: 20).

Isa has no clear conception of the road on which his feet are set, but Hazil sees it clearly, and his enthusiastic sense of dedication is expressed in the composition of which he says: 'This music sings the struggle of man as man . . . For me the individual is an end, not the means to an end . . . This music is my life. This is the revolution we have begun. But the revolution is only a means to attain freedom, and freedom is only a means to enrich the happiness and nobility of human life'.

Isa remains unenthusiastic. So far from glorying in his invividuality, he prefers to find safety in the anonymity of the herd, where there is protection against shocks and bruises. All the same, it is he who makes an inspired suggestion for the orchestration of Hazil's work, and is aware of the role of the drum, resounding through Indonesian history since the arrival in the East Indies of the Dong Song bronze culture, half a millennium before the birth of Christ. Then, its reverberations were the vehicle enabling the souls of the shaman to ascend in trance to the spirit world, and Isa suggests using the drum in a similar way to 'create the rhythmic pattern that will produce the atmosphere we want; then we can gradually fade it until it is just a background to the music'. His solution is surprisingly suggestive of the Beethoven violin concerto.

One could go even further in the interpretation of Hazil's music and see the melody as epitomising the human quest for happiness and the drum as the part of Indonesian man in that search involving loneliness, fear,

9

joy and terror. This recalls the Confession of Faith: 'This Indonesian culture will be determined by the manifold responses made on our part to stimuli from every corner of the globe', and an open, rather than closed, sense of nationalism with confidence in its own dignity and value remains Lubis's fundamental conviction. A heightened sense of the underlying meaning of the book is gained if we think for a moment of the astonishing dialogue between the drum and violin in the cadenza to the first movement of the Beethoven violin concerto, and then turn to Isa and Hazil, as they take violin and drum in turn in playing their newly-composed work. In spite of flaws arising from the haste with which it was written, the novel has an organic unity which enables it to be seen in musical terms. The basic motifs of fear, self-knowledge, impotence, lightning, the road, are all woven together and sustained by the pervading drumbeats—the rolls of thunder, the pounding truck wheels in the empty streets, and the thudding of Isa's heart, leading to an almost symphonic apotheosis in his final release from fear.

The great themes of the book find their intellectual, discursive formulation in the writings of the outstanding Sudjatmoko, who wrote in his major essay on National Culture: 'The reduction of Man to a tool designed exclusively for the service of Race or State . . . is totally alien to the Indonesian personality . . . the noblest vocation for art and the artist in the conclusion of the Indonesian Revolution is to preserve the humanity of Indonesian Man, to ensure that he is not submerged in a welter of schemes and plans, to ensure that he does not become a mere statistic, a tool, even for the best of motives (intentions)'. Hazil is expressing the same ideas when he says: 'For me, the individual is an end, not the means to an end . . . the State is only a means . . . the individual must not be subordinated to the State'.

Such sentiments may provoke a wry smile in the light of the adulation of Sukarno between 1957 and 1965, and the attempt to subordinate every aspect of Indonesian life to the Indonesian Personality and State. But the point is that Lubis, as early as 1950, foresaw the danger of such a development, and that in 1959 Sudjatmoko had the courage and ingenuity to turn Sukarno's own concept of 'National Personality' against its creator. When Lubis was imprisoned it was for his commitment to Universal Humanism—by then regarded as decadent, socially unproductive and bourgeois—and his insistence that he was first a man, a free individual, and then an Indonesian.

In the western literary tradition, this book finds an echo for me in Steinbeck's *The Moon is Down*. Theme and setting are approximately parallel—simple folk in a community harassed by enemy occupation gradually develop a response to the threat to their freedom. Orden, the mayor, the man on whom responsibility falls, gradually and uncertainly gropes his way to the position he must take. He, like Isa, is a man who knows fear and in his own way learns to master it: 'You know, Doctor,' he says to his friend, Winter, 'I am a little man, and this is a little town, but there must be a spark in little men that can burst into flame. I am afraid, I am terribly afraid, and I thought of all the things I might do to save my own life, and then that went away, and sometimes now I feel a kind of exultation, as though I were bigger and better than I am . . .'

Both books are concerned with the integrity of man

the individual, not man as an anonymous member of the herd. When Orden says: 'Free men cannot start a war, but once it is started they can fight on in defeat. Herd men, followers of a leader, cannot do that, and so it is always the herd men who win battles and the free men who win wars'; he is echoing the accents of Hazil: 'The struggle of man is not that of the herd; it is not the bark of jackals hunting in a pack, but the bark, the growl, the pain and sharp cry of the individual jackal in his struggle for life'. Yet there is one profound difference in theme: Lubis's book is more genuinely concerned with the problems of man as man. Steinbeck harnessed the traditions of Western Civilisation from Socrates onwards to the war effort against Hitler, regarding the Norwegian villagers at this period in their history as light-bearers marshalled against the powers of Hitlerian darkness. Lubis did not write in support of the Indonesian revolution, which for him is but part of a much greater struggle—the pilgrimage of man to realise the dignity of the human spirit. Accordingly, he feels no compulsion to claim for it any immaculate qualities. As with any human movement, it houses evil alongside of good, and characters such as the monstrous Ontong and the paroxysms of pointless killing Lubis describes, were as much part of it as Hazil's noble idealism.

The new literatures of the developing nations are concerned with the same types of experience, and their writers are beset with the same challenges, temptations, and pressures. When the self-exiled South African writer Ezekiel Mphahlele writes that enemies have associated him with 'colonialism, neo-colonialism and imperialism', the student of modern Indonesian literature feels that he has been here before. And when he goes on:

'We in South Africa have for the last three hundred years of oppression been engaged in a bloody struggle against white supremacy—to assert our *human* and not African dignity. This latter we have always taken for granted,' he touches on something crucial in the psychological and literary development of the Afro-Asian countries which he pinpoints with his exclamation: 'Why should *la littérature engagée* be so spoiled as to want to be judged by different standards from those that have been tested by tradition? Why should it be afraid of being judged against the social context that gives rise to it and run for cover behind the black mask?' For 'black mask' (negritude) we can substitute Sukarno's mythologisation of the Indonesian personality, Mao Tse Tung's 'workers and peasants' and all sectional foci of loyalty which regard a party truth as superior to human moral truth.

That *A Road with No End* concerns man as man, not as Indonesian or Dutch, despite the pressures of the times when it was written, gives it an importance even greater than its intrinsic literary merit, because the message of Lubis, like that of Mphahlele, is that one of mankind's greatest needs is the courage not to shelter behind colour, race, or creed to conceal real or imagined inadequacies. This is what gives relevance to the quotation from Jules Romains that precedes the book: 'What must we have in order to be free from fear?' From what kind of fear? Not least from the timid insecurity that feels the compulsion to seek shelter behind such amorphous concepts as negritude, national personality, and the like.

The kinship that one finds between the ideas of Lubis and Sudjatmoko is explicable in that Lubis, too, is an intellectual. In a letter to me he explained that his decision to devote his principal energies to journalism rather than literature was the result of careful thought and quite deliberate. He felt that in this way he could communicate to a far wider public his ideals of democracy and individual responsibility. If his record has shown him a man of courage, he admits, too, that he knows fear, and that he was indeed fearful of the results of his editorials, awaiting the moment when his political enemies should act to still his pen. The tensions, the scarcely balanced complex of contrary forces in Indonesia, is exceedingly complex. For Lubis, no amount of special pleading and reference to historical circumstances can gainsay his principle that whatever problem it faces, a nation cannot have faith in itself unless it has faith in the liberty of the individual; for men who do not believe in themselves put themselves in the power of others to find an illusion of security. The essence of his message is that every individual must discover the courage to walk a man's road according to his own conscience and in response to his responsibilities, even if it means walking alone.

Lubis then, even as a journalist, has kept faith with the vision enshrined in this novel. Yet is it too much to hope that in an enriched maturity he will return to literature for its own sake, to take his readers with him a stage further along the Road with No End?

Anthony H. Johns
Professor of Indonesian Languages and Literatures
Australian National University
Canberra

What must we have in order to be free from fear?

JULES ROMAINS

I

Drizzle brought darkness swiftly down. Lightning, accompanied by deep rolls of thunder, flashed all round the horizon, the momentary brightness followed by an even denser darkness. The roads were empty and deserted apart from a few people hurrying to shelter from the rain and the threatening atmosphere which had long hung over the city.

The wheels of a patrol truck filled with hard-faced soldiers drummed through the empty streets. It turned to the right, went straight ahead, then to the left, then to the right, then on and on through the silent, empty and deserted streets, travelling through a night of dark drizzle on a course endlessly turning—a road with no end.

DJAKARTA, SEPTEMBER 1946. MORNING.
Three children were playing in Gang Djaksa. Three

17

children with a kite. One kept the string taut, another stood on tiptoe, holding it up high so that its tail was in the air; the third gave instructions. 'Wrong, wrong. The wind's from there. Change places.' he shouted. They obeyed. 'Right, let it go now,' he shouted again. 'Quick!'

From Gang Kebon Sirih Wetan came another child, bigger and stronger than the three playing. His stride and bearing marked him as the local bully. He was holding a stick he had broken off a nangka* tree. He stood at the end of the alley and looked left and right, and seeing the three children at their game, smiled and strolled in their direction.

I'll take Djudjuh's kite, he thought contentedly. The moment the idea entered his head he looked round in case a mother was in the offing, watching the children. The coast was clear. He strode towards them.

At Pak Damrah's stall six people were drinking coffee. It was hardly a stall, only eight roof strips supported on four bamboo poles stuck into the ground at the side of the road. Every morning Pak Damrah brought his wares to do business at this little stall where he sold rice, roast peanuts, curried fish, spices, fried bananas and hot coffee. Four of them were peons of the City Office at Kebon Sirih. They stopped there every morning on their way to work for a cup of coffee and one or two fried bananas.† The others were a pedicab driver stopping for a morning snack—his pedicab parked beside the little stall, and a rag and bone man about to set out on his morning rounds. A knee protruded from the hole in his sarong.

*Jackfruit—resembling the West Indian breadfruit.
†A typical underprivileged breakfast in Djakarta.

'Yesterday the Sikhs turned the Tanah Tinggi precinct upside down,' he mumbled, his mouth full of fried banana.

The pedicab driver sipping his hot coffee, wiped his mouth with a dark and grimy left arm, and said, 'Yes, I was there. It was three hours before we could leave.' The rag and bone man looked at him and laughed briefly.

'Do you know?'—he asked secretively—the four peons about to move on to the City Office sat down again—the intonation of the rag and bone man suggested an exciting story.

Pak Damrah broke up a few more pieces of wood, and put them into his portable stove. He arranged them carefully, one by one, the muscles of his hand standing out against the skin. He had no interest in exciting stories.

'I helped three youths at Tanah Tinggi yesterday'— the man went on. 'They hid two revolvers and five grenades in my junk basket, and I went and sat by the Sikhs' truck until the search was over.' The rag and bone man looked around him proudly.

'Weren't you afraid?' asked one of the peons.

'Afraid?' he answered rhetorically, and looking at the faces around him one by one. He knew no one would believe him if he said he hadn't been afraid. He decided to tell the truth.

'Course. I was scared to death. Not of the Sikhs but of the youths. They threatened to kill me if I didn't hide their weapons. When the Sikhs had gone they came and took them back. Only then did I breathe freely.'

'Then?' pressed the pedicab driver.

'They gave me a tip of five rupiah,' he replied and

tossed the money onto the small table to pay for his coffee and fried bananas. The four peons got up and moved towards their office. Pak Damrah opened his table drawer to get change for the rag and bone man. The pedicab driver sipped his coffee.

Baba* Tan was sitting in a chair in front of his stall and puffed on a long bamboo pipe. A woman carrying a child on her hip stopped in front of the stall and looked at him. Baba Tan paid no attention, or at least pretended not to see her. She was a little doubtful, wondering whether to carry on her way or to stop. At length she turned and entered the stall. 'Give me two litres of rice' she said to Baba Tan's child standing at the counter. The child packed the rice and placed it on the table in front of her.

'Six rupiah!'

'It's gone up again. The day before yesterday it was only two and a half,' countered the woman.

'Rice is scarce now,' the child replied, defending the price.

'Put it on the slate,' she replied, reaching for the packet.

'You can't have any more credit,' said Baba Tan from the door to the stall; he had been listening for a while.

'But I'm a regular customer.'

'Yes, but now we're all hard up. Me too,' said Baba Tan. 'I can't give you any more credit. Impossible.'

The woman drew back her hand and stood silent. Where can I borrow money, she thought. She was annoyed. Ah, Isa, perhaps!

'Put this on one side. I'll get some money,' she said. And quickly went out of the shop and turned onto the main road.

*A common form of address for Indonesian Chinese men.

She had gone only a few paces when there was a sudden roar of truck engines and people, startled, were shouting: 'Watch out! Watch out!' one to another. Before she had a chance to run, two trucks filled with steel-helmeted soldiers came from the direction of Kebon Sirih and turned into Gang Djaksa. She hurried back into the stall.

The four peons had almost reached the intersection of Gang Djaksa with Kebon Sirih, when the chorus of 'Watch out!' commenced. Without thinking they leapt for shelter towards the yard of a house at the edge of the road. Seeing their movement, the soldiers on the truck opened fire. Rifle and sten-gun shots rent the air of the deserted street. Two of them were halted in their steps as though seized by a giant invisible hand, and sank to the ground, their faces buried in the dust. The other two ran on and disappeared behind a house. The truck sped on. The children playing with the kite had no chance to escape. When the truck reached the spot where they had been playing, they had only got to Pak Damrah's stall.

The pedicab driver and the rag and bone man leapt up to flee. Pak Damrah was frozen to his bench. The soldiers on the truck continued firing, aiming at anyone they saw running. The pedicab driver slumped down with a leg wound. One of the children collapsed without a cry, writhed once or twice, then lay very still in the dust of the road.

The woman carrying the child ran back into the store. Baba Tan and his child had long taken cover in the hencoop behind it, heedless that it was unattended.

Three minutes later the trucks appeared at the intersection of Gang Djaksa and Djalan Asam Lama. The soldiers on both of them were still firing to the left and right, screaming and hurling insults. 'Croak, you dogs of Sukarno. Is it freedom you want? Here, take it!' and the stens and rifles were fired in all directions.

The woman carrying her child hurried off and disappeared into one of the alleys off Kebon Sirih Wetan. Baba Tan with his child and their family stayed hidden in the hencoop.

A quarter of an hour later, since no further trucks had appeared, youths armed with bamboo spears, patrolling behind fences, houses, behind privies and kitchens, gradually showed themselves. They moved one by one along the alleys and a few people gradually plucked up the courage to come out of Gang Djaksa and Kebon Sirih Wetan.

Some ran to telephone for ambulances. Others gathered around Pak Damrah's little stall. One picked up the child which had been shot and laid him at the side of the road, the string of his kite still clasped in his grubby little hand. He lay motionless.

Pak Damrah had not been hurt but was speechless with shock. To the questions which poured on him from every direction, he could only respond with a blank look on his pale face.

A few youths carrying bamboo spears came running. They were followed by another with a revolver who asked the wounded pedicab driver who had done the shooting and how many were involved. Blood was flowing from the wound in the man's leg and he lay groaning heedless of the youth's questions. He turned away and directed a few people to move the bodies of the two peons to the side of the road. They were still alive but badly wounded. Their threadbare green jackets were red, soaked with congealing blood. Both were in pain.

A little later a Red Cross ambulance arrived to pick up the wounded man and the dead child.

'I'll telephone the Antara News Office,' said the youth with the revolver to no one in particular.

When the shooting at Gang Djaksa first broke the silence of the morning, Isa, a teacher, was walking to his school at Tanah Abang. For a moment a pang of anxiety passed through his mind as to the safety of his wife and his son. Ah, Fatima will be careful, he thought; I've told her not to leave the house. The shout 'Watch out! Watch out!' was taken up through the quarters situated around Laan Holle and Djalan Asam Lama and these thoroughfares too were soon deserted. Isa had to ask for shelter in the house of strangers, but they were kindly people who welcomed him into their home.

He crouched on the verandah beside the owner peeping from behind the windows at the deserted main road. His breathlessness from running was easing but fear had not yet left his heart. Djalan Asam Lama covered with white dust, filled with pot holes, was empty. A mangy dog crossed the road in front of the house.

The owner's wife moved to leave the room, but her husband waved her back.

For about five minutes they were huddled together. The road was still deserted. Isa felt that he should introduce himself. He turned to the owner and said with a shy smile.

'My name is Isa. I'm a teacher at the Tanah Abang School.'

'Oh! I am Semedi, from the Department of Finance,' replied the owner, shaking Isa's hand.

Across the road opposite the house, two youths armed

23

with rifles were crawling for cover behind the white wall and the Chinese myrtle fence of green.

'Someone's coming,' Semedi whispered. Isa craned his neck to look out of the window and watched the two youths crawling behind the fence.

From the house next door, another youth leapt into the yard of the house where they were hiding. He was armed only with a revolver. Seeing the pair of them behind the window he ducked towards them and said:

'The Sikhs' truck is at the end of the road. They're coming from the Tanah Abang Bukit end. Be careful.'

Before he finished speaking, the cry 'Watch out! Watch out!' echoed and re-echoed. The youth with a revolver leapt back to the middle of the road, ducked back across it and disappeared behind the Chinese myrtle fence to crouch next to the two youths with rifles.

Isa now heard the sound of a truck and he shifted himself with Semedi to peep from a window facing the direction from which it came. It stopped three houses from them.

Isa turned and looked to where the three youths were hiding and waiting. He wanted to know what they would do. They had not yet fired.

Isa could not describe his feelings when he looked back and saw the Indian soldiers jump down from the truck. There was a hollow feeling in the pit of his stomach and his chest felt constricted, not from running but from the struggle to control himself. He looked out of the corner of his eye towards Semedi. He was no longer there. Isa was alone on the verandah. For a moment he felt an impulse to run, but quickly realised there was nowhere he could go. The Indians were only three houses away.

Suddenly one of the youths with a rifle fired. Isa saw the dust spurt up near the feet of one of the Indians. He'd missed. The soldiers quickly scattered and threw themselves on the ground looking for cover. One rolled into a ditch and then another leapt behind a low wall as they fired in the direction of the hiding-place. Isa watched them crawl backwards until they had cover from the wall of the house and then rapidly disappear behind it. The soldier behind the low wall continued firing rapidly while the three men who had thrown themselves flat on the road close to the truck, suddenly leapt up and ran bent double towards the place where the three youths had been hiding.

Isa forgot for a moment that he was in danger, so fascinated was he by what was happening before his eyes. He only realised that he too might be shot when suddenly he heard the explosion of a rifle from the house next door, followed by a cry of pain and the sound of heavy running footsteps.

Before he had a chance to think what to do, the front door was suddenly kicked open and in the doorway stood a huge Sikh soldier, the rifle he had just fired in his hands with smoke curling from the muzzle. 'God have mercy on us!' Isa exclaimed to himself, startled and overcome with fear. It flashed through his mind that now he was to be shot dead; and he thought of his wife and Salim who was four.

'Hands up!' ordered the Sikh fiercely. Before Isa could get to his feet and raise his hands the back door was kicked open and three other soldiers entered. Isa stood up and raised his hands. Quickly a soldier strode forward and searched him. Isa was unarmed and he was ordered to stand in the middle of the room. Then a soldier pounded on the bedroom door and a moment later Semedi, his wife and two small children came out. They were trembling and white with terror. They too were searched. Isa was filled with fear and loathing when he saw the coarse hairy hands of the soldier searching Semedi's wife. He handled her roughly, resting his hand longer than was necessary on her breast. Her husband looked away, unwilling to see her abused.

Isa thought of his own wife for a moment and asked himself what he would do if their house were raided, and if coarse soldiers searched her. Would he resist? He didn't think of it long because in his heart he knew that he too would not dare resist. The fear of death would get the better of him too.

The four soldiers went out by the back door. A moment later there was a whistle; Isa and Semedi looked again from the back window. They saw the Indian soldiers reassemble, climb back onto the truck and the truck driven off swiftly until it disappeared in the direction of Laan Holle.

Isa turned to the owner of the house beside him and he said, 'I think it's all clear now. Thank you very much for your kindness. Now I must go on to school.'

And saying *Merdeka** he left the house. On the road in front of the house next door, people were gathered around a man lying on the ground. Isa could not restrain his curiosity and went into the yard pressing his way through them. A middle-aged Chinese was lying prone, blood flowing from his side. He was moaning with pain, and as Isa arrived a Chinese woman came running from the house with a piece of white cloth. One

*This revolutionary greeting 'Freedom' has none of the necessary overtones in English, and is left untranslated.

of the group took the cloth from the sobbing woman and tried to staunch the bleeding. The woman crouched on the ground and stroked his head. His forehead and face were covered in sweat:

'Has the ambulance been called?' someone asked. 'Yes,' came a reply. 'It'll be here in a moment.'

A few suggested lifting the man indoors but someone said. 'Don't! Leave him here until the ambulance comes.'

Isa got up, hardly knowing what to do. He heard voices but couldn't grasp what they were saying. 'He was running, otherwise he wouldn't have been shot!'

'Who wouldn't run,' said another voice, 'at the sight of the Sikhs!'

The Chinese woman waited, crying with shock and fear at the sight of her husband lying on the ground covered in blood.

If I had been shot how would it be with my wife and my child, thought Guru Isa. A feeling of disquiet rose within him as he imagined himself lying on the ground covered with blood moaning with pain. Such a sight pained his gentle heart. He felt it a violation of human dignity.

He was startled from the stream of his thoughts by a shout: 'Here's the ambulance!'

An ambulance stopped at the edge of the road in front of them. Four girls in uniform leapt down. A youth wearing a Red Cross armband helped by the driver brought out a stretcher. They made way for the four nurses, placed the stretcher at the side of the wounded Chinese, then waited. The nurses got to work quickly.

'An emergency dressing first,' ordered the nurse in charge.

They placed the Chinese on the stretcher and Isa and the others were about to help lift it into the ambulance when suddenly the terrifying 'Watch out! Watch out!' re-echoed from all directions. They wasted no time because hardly had the shout 'Watch out! Watch out!' died away than the sound of a truck was heard from the direction of Tanah Abang. Someone urged the nurses to run to the back of the house, crying 'Hide there'. Isa and the others ran after him to the back of the house, crawling through the bamboo fence, and after they had passed several alleys he stopped.

'It's safe here. They never come in as far as this.'

Isa, unaccustomed to running, stood panting. The nurses made to return to go back to the wounded Chinese but people restrained them.

'Don't,' they said. 'The Sikhs have no respect for the Red Cross.'

Those in the alley urged them to come further in.

'You'd better sit here,' they pressed. Isa felt moved at the sight of the good nature of his people who, despite danger, did not forget courtesy and kindness. He sat on a bench beside them.

This was the first time he had had a chance to get a better look at them. They were all young—between eighteen and twenty-one.

One of them looked towards him and smiled as though to coax him not to feel afraid.

'We are used to this,' she said pleasantly. 'Last night we had to sleep at the office because we didn't finish work until one o'clock. In the clash at Kramat alone there were twelve victims and at Sawah Besar there were six.'

The one in charge got up and ordered them to go back.

'We can't leave him there,' she said.

What a sense of duty, thought Isa proudly. He looked at the Chinese woman who had run after them and was now crouching at the edge of the alley, whimpering to herself. One of the girls went to her and took her along. The youth and the ambulance driver ran ahead to see if there were still any Sikhs.

They gave a signal that all was quiet and the nurses together with Isa and the wounded man's wife and several other men from the village came closer, bent double. They stopped at the bamboo fence behind the house of the wounded Chinese. Semedi who had just come out of the back door of his house saw Isa and waved to him.

'Go on,' he called. 'It's all right now. The Sikhs only wanted to move the Eurasian family next door. People say they felt threatened here and requested to be moved to the 10th Battalion's precinct. The Sikhs came to give them protection.'

For a moment the thought passed through Isa's mind —why had someone to be killed, just for that.

The nurses hurried towards the wounded man left lying on the stretcher. His wife put her arms round his shoulders, wailing as though afraid that were her husband taken he would never return again. The nurse, who had accompanied her, tried to soothe her saying, 'Don't cry. He'll be all right. He'll be able to come home tomorrow.'

Isa didn't believe it. The man looked on the point of death.

As the youth and the ambulance driver raised the stretcher two large lorries filled with Sikhs passed the house leaving a cloud of dust behind them.

The nurses followed the stretcher to the ambulance and a moment later it, too, disappeared in a cloud of dust churned up by its wheels as it headed for the Central Hospital.

Isa looked around but there was no one he knew. Semedi had gone indoors again. The road was still deserted but two or three people were beginning to appear in front of their houses looking up and down the road. Isa summoned up his courage and walked out in the direction of his school keeping close to the fence.

He was very disturbed. He had not got over the shock of being chased, of seeing a human being shot and blood spilt. And all, he thought uncomprehendingly, to pick up a family that wanted to move. He could not understand why, to move house, someone had to be shot dead. The possibility even, that people could act in such a way had not entered his simple kindly heart. The wounded man's blood which had spurted out and was drying on his shirt made him feel fear and nausea. People outside their houses asked him what had happened, but he could not answer. He was totally absorbed in his own confusion.

When he reached the school he saw that many children were absent. Two teachers who were already there when he arrived, were getting ready to leave.

'Why are you going home?' asked Isa.

'Only five children of our class have come—only to be expected; there's been a clash.'

Isa nodded and quickly went to his classroom. It was empty. He took from his desk drawer the exercise books he had to mark. He had barely done three when he felt weary. He pushed the pile to one side on the table. He doodled with the pen still wet with red ink, scratching on the blotting paper covering the table.

For a while the pen marks multiplied until suddenly, startled, he hurled the pen to the floor. His etchings in red ink reminded him of the wounded man.

Isa buried his face in his hands and groaned quietly. He didn't realise it, but he was going through a delayed reaction to the fear he had so far managed to suppress. Now his fears came to the surface taking on various forms. The days ahead were obscure and frightening. The safety of his wife and his child; the continually rising cost of living—his inadequate salary. There was two months owing at the store. The rent on his house was three months in arrears. His wife's jewelry had been pawned. Isa laid his head on the table, his mind in a turmoil.

Mr. Kamarudin, retired Chairman of the District Council, that morning was sitting sipping coffee on the back terrace of his big house in Kebon Sirih. He was old. He was sixty. And like many old people, he was fussy and liked to show his authority. He had just scolded his servant because there was not enough sugar in his coffee. He liked his coffee with plenty of sugar. It had to be sweet. That morning apparently the sugar had run out; there was only a teaspoonful left in the jar, and the servant had not bought more.

When the shooting broke out at Gang Djaksa, Kamarudin was just taking another sip of his coffee to drown his anger in the hot fluid which scalded his tongue. It helped a little, warmed both his blood and his body which was becoming cold. The sound startled him, the

31

coffee cup in his hand shook, and a drop of coffee was spilt soiling his pyjamas.*

'Hell,' he groused. 'Why does there have to be shooting every morning! The world is coming to an end! Everyone is mad!'

He sighed and thought of the time before the war when he was still Chairman of the District Council. Life was easy then, especially for people such as he, senior government officials.

He put down the cup again and slapped the table with his hand, wrinkled but still strong. A youth ran out, slamming the door hard behind him in his haste. He had a revolver in his hand. Before he had reached the door Kamarudin stood up and shouted:

'Hazil'

The youth stopped running and turned round by the door.

'Where are you going?' called Kamarudin.

Not giving his son a chance to answer, Kamarudin went on.

'Do you want to join in the battle? How many times have I forbidden you? You are to have nothing to do with the war! Do you think that you can win any victories with just a revolver?' Apparently he remembered something. 'So you still haven't got rid of that pistol. Didn't I tell you a week ago. Obstinate child! Do you want to be killed!'

Mr. Kamarudin, sixty years old, former Chairman of the District Council, was only too aware that his son did not obey him. He felt extremely angry; to which was added the sense of frustration that this morning

*Pyjamas in Indonesia are a garment to relax at home in; they are not used exclusively for sleeping.

there had not been enough sugar in his coffee. He rose from his chair and walked towards his son.

'Give me that revolver,' he ordered.

Hazil took a step backward.

'No, father. We need weapons to fight for freedom.'

'Freedom! Rubbish!' shouted Kamarudin. 'You youths are all mad. Do you think that we can defeat the Dutch? You are lunatics to rebel.'

Mr. Kamarudin moved to snatch the revolver from his son's hand. But Hazil quickly turned and ran; and as he reached the gate of the house, looking to left and right to examine the empty road, his father's cry followed him:

'Hazil, come back!'

In that shout was hidden an emotion greater than anger. It was the love of a father for his son, and fear of the realisation that his son had gone to face danger of death. Hidden in that cry also was Kamarudin's own fear, a fear he kept deeply buried within his heart; fear at the sight of the changing times, and changes in his son—changes he could not understand. He did not understand why people would not accept Dutch rule again. If the Dutch returned everything would return to normal. He himself would get his pension again and perhaps even be re-employed—he knew there was a great shortage of staff in the Government—and the comfort and respect which he had had before would be his again. He had spoken of this many times with his contemporaries and they all agreed with him.

Seeing that the road was empty Hazil swiftly crossed it and went into the front yard of the house facing his own, then hurriedly ran to the back and disappeared in the complex behind the main road. As he ran through the narrow alleys the sound of shooting at Gang Djaksa faded away in the distance.

A youth, hiding behind a fence, holding a bamboo spear saw him pass. 'Hazil,' he called.

Hazil stopped running and looked round.

'You, Mid!' he said. 'Where is it?'

'Just by Gang Djaksa,' the youth replied. He whistled and from behind the house came three other youths, all with bamboo spears. They looked jealously and with pride at the revolver Hazil was holding. 'Let's go to Gang Djaksa' suggested Hazil.

The youths' courage rose to see that they had a revolver between them. When they arrived at Gang Djaksa the truckcarrying the NI CA* soldiers shooting in all directions had already gone and they saw a small crowd around Pak Damrah's little stall.

'Perhaps it'sPak Da mrah!' exclaimed one of them.

Hazil asked the prone pedicab driver who had done the shooting and how many. Blood was still seeping from the wound in his leg and he moaned.

*Netherland Indies Civil Administration.

2

As the old dusty wall-clock struck eleven, Isa raised his head and laid his pen and pencil on the table. He had finished marking his pupils' exercises. He put the exercise books together and placed them carefully back into his desk drawer. As he did so he caught sight of four packages of new ones—fifty in each bundle, still unopened.

Isa listened carefully. The school was silent. The other teachers had gone home. His head was aching. Some had taken their work to finish at home. Exercise books were expensive on the open market. At home there was no money. If he took a bundle, he thought no one would know—and with the money he could buy rice. A feeling of embarrassment stole through him as this thought entered his mind.

That the desire to steal should ever enter my mind! he thought, ashamed of himself. He swiftly closed the desk drawer and locked it, as though afraid of being tempted if he looked at them for too long. For a few moments he sat resting his chin on his hand. Then he took a glass standing upside down on his desk. It was grimy as though rarely washed with soap. Isa stood up and went outside to the tap next to the back wall of the class. His stomach rumbled because he had had nothing to eat. He filled the glass, raised it high as though proposing a toast in wine, and he drank the water in large gulps. His Adam's apple rose and fell visibly with every gulp. He filled the glass again and drank it down, then half-filled it, dipped his finger in it and twisted it around the length of the glass, shook the water about vigorously and emptied it onto the grass. He held the glass up to the light—it's clean, he thought to himself. He walked back towards the classroom, his left hand patting his stomach: 'You're full now. No more playing up', said the hand to his empty stomach—he'd taken nothing since early morning, and his stomach fell silent. He felt a slight return of energy to his listless body and realised his headache had gone. Just hunger, perhaps, he thought, fortunately not illness. The thought heartened him. His step was firmer as he went into the classroom. It seemed no longer empty but full of pupils awaiting his arrival. His vitality did not diminish at the sight of the class still silent and empty. He began to whistle—a children's song with a simple melody he had composed for his class—truth is simplicity and simplicity is truth, thought Isa. He opened the cupboard and took out his violin case. It was old and, at the ends, the lacquered cloth cover was peeling off.

He took out the violin and rubbed the belly with his

handkerchief. For a moment he recalled the time when he had entered the Teachers' College at Bandung; then how he had become a teacher in the years before the Second World War. A time still not so far distant. Then, he was still young. He was thirty-one. Now, he was already thirty-five. Why did he say 'already'? Wasn't thirty-five a good age? One was not too young to do things one would regret having done after doing them, and not too old to be unable to do those things which, if left undone, later would give rise to disappointment, to regrets and the question, 'Why didn't I do that?'.

Perhaps it is the hardships of the Japanese occupation and the past months which make me feel older than I should, he thought to himself. He smiled, looking at his violin.

He placed it under his chin and began to play the song he had composed. He played it several times, then, unconsciously began to play an altogether different melody. The melodies he still remembered from the time he had learned the violin—snatches of melodies of Schubert and Chopin. He liked best those of Chopin. There was something in Chopin's music which set his heart trembling, which awoke emotions he himself could not analyse clearly.

While he was playing his thoughts wandered, sometimes to his wife, to his empty purse, to the rice which had to be bought.

Could Fatima get credit at the store, he asked himself. Thinking of his wife led his mind to Tien, a contemporary at the Teachers' College. He had liked, loved Tien when a student. It's a long time since I've heard from her, he thought. Where is she now? He smiled to himself, thinking of the moments with Tien which were past, never to return again. They were gone, and he could recall them without disturbing his thoughts or feelings—indeed he found a kind of satisfaction in his memories. Isa smiled again and stopped playing for a moment. He resined the bow. He thought of his father who had died just after his marriage. Thinking of his father led his thoughts back to his first meeting with Fatima, daughter of an uncle he had not seen for a long time as they lived far apart. He was attracted to her at once, and quickly forgot Tien. Isa smiled to himself. His thoughts pleased him. He took up his violin again, and began to play a melody of Chopin.

What am I thinking of, thought Isa, all at once surprised at himself—I'm thinking too much of the past. Suddenly his mind returned to the clash at Djalan Asam Lama. He saw before his eyes the wounded Chinese. He was bleeding. He imagined himself shot and unpleasant feelings troubled his mind. Isa shrugged his shoulders, attempting to dissipate the feeling. He shook his head violently.

As with most people, during the first days of the revolution, Isa had not fully analysed his own position, his responsibility or his work. Up to the present he had let himself be carried along by the current. By the current of popular emotion—the current of thoughts and words flowing from all kinds of people. He, too, had become a member of the precinct guard. Indeed, because of his position as a teacher, he had become a Deputy-Chairman of the People's Security Committee and an adviser to the Body for Public Safety.

But today was the first time he had met face to face the hard and sharp outlines of the revolution—the spilling of blood, human blood. Isa would have felt hurt had anyone said to him that what he was feeling now was fear. He was in fact afraid but to himself he would not admit that he was afraid.

Since he had passed the age when children quarrel, Isa had never used violence towards anyone. Neither had he ever suffered physical violence directed against himself. His fists had never clenched to strike anyone, neither had a blow ever bruised his face. Isa was truly a man of peace, a man who loved peace and welcomed peace. His experience of violence was limited to what he had seen in the cinema or read in books.

There are many people who have never raised their voices in anger but who often in their dreams see themselves as heroes, as champion boxers, as marksmen, as detectives, daring police officers and the like. But not Isa. Never, even in his dreams, had he imagined himself using violence against another.

Isa did not believe in violence. Because of this, over the past few years his view of life had gradually become confused. The violence displayed by the Japanese hurt him deeply. During the Japanese occupation he had not felt able to share the enthusiasm of those joining the Keibodan or Peta and especially when he heard people idolising Kido butai, or Djibaku tai,* as a rule he either remained silent or withdrew. It was to him as though they were speaking a foreign language which he did not understand, without significance to his emotions.

Isa looked at the calendar on the wall. In a few months we'll celebrate our wedding anniversary, he

---

*Keibodan (Civilian Guard, Vigilance Corps), Peta (Abbreviation for the Japanese-sponsored Volunteer Army of Defenders of the Fatherland), Kido butai (Mobile Corps), Djibaku tai (Suicide Corps).

thought, on the fifth of January. Isa recalled his wedding night. He smiled to himself, momentarily. Then his face grew overcast. He remembered the occasion six months after their marriage. It was the first time he had not been able to serve his wife. For some time he had felt that his virility was ebbing—before he married this had often happened to him—like water draining from a leaking tin. The next night he was again impotent. His wife's expression was contemptuous. The following night was the same and so on, until his mind became disturbed; so it had been up to the present; and now his wife was indifferent to him. But they still preserved their marriage. He had been to a doctor, and the doctor had told him that his physical impotence resulted from a kind of psychological impotence, the only remedy for which lay in his own mind or in some external event which could free him from a temperament oppressed by a sense of inadequacy.

So it was with his personality. From that time many major changes had occurred in his personality without his realising it. He knew that his wife had suffered during these last few years. She had been able to restrain the natural longing implanted in her youthful body full of the fire of life. Even so, on occasions her longing overwhelmed her. Yet never could Isa satisfy her needs.

His mental anguish was intense. Yet even though now after all these years, with every treatment unsuccessful, it was still suppressed, he did not realise that this anguish and disappointment was etched into his subconscious affecting his outlook, his mind, his attitudes to the world about him. Isa was not aware of this.

When his wife had decided to adopt a child a year ago there had almost been a major quarrel. At first he had objected, thinking of the additional expense and the burden to their household this would entail . . . then his wife had said, 'I cannot hope for a child from you.'

He had bowed his head, full of shame at the helplessness of his manhood. He said nothing further. Thus Salim, a small boy of four, came into their lives to fill the place of the child he should have been able to give. But deep within his subconscious that child was a symbol of his impotence.

Isa was unaware of these feelings. All his sense of disappointment bordering on despair, was expressed in other forms.

He stopped playing his violin. His fragile happiness, springing from a stomach filled with two glasses of cold water had fled, like glowing ashes swiftly grown cold. The room felt overcast.

A light rain began to fall, whispering against the roof. Isa yearned to see his class full again with mischievous, uproarious children.

He shook his head to dispel the thoughts filling his heart with regret and uncertainty. He forced himself to play his violin again. He played the Heroic Polonaise of Chopin—a melody like the outburst of a storm, of emotions in frenzy. The gloomy schoolroom vanished in a whirl about him. Then he began to play the Nocturne in E Flat—a melody full of eternal calm and beauty.

'Isa! Isa!'

Isa did not hear his name called.

'Isa!'

He still did not hear.

Not until the new arrival tapped his shoulder did he realise that there was someone else in the classroom.

Startled, he looked around. 'Saleh', he exclaimed, relieved. He did not know why he should have been startled or felt relieved.

'There aren't any children,' said Saleh. He wasn't asking a question, only stating what he had seen with his own eyes.

'I was late myself. When I got here the school was empty—perhaps because of the clash at Djalan Asam Lama,' replied Isa.

'Our other colleagues?'

'Hamid and Zabir have gone home.'

'My lodgings were searched. They only finished an hour ago.'

'Was anyone arrested?'

'No.'

They were silent. Saleh took the glass from the table and walked out to the tap, as he walked saying, 'As long as I don't get a chill because of this drizzle.'

Isa remained without answering.

'It's a long time since I heard you play the violin like that,' said Saleh as he came back in, a half-filled glass of water in his hand. Isa smiled a little. Should he tell the confused thoughts that had passed through his mind that morning?

'Chopin is better played on the piano,' he said. Saleh would laugh at me if I told him all my doubts and anxieties, he thought.

'I enjoy hearing you talk about music,' said Saleh. 'Carry on.'

'Play?'

'Yes'.

'This morning I saw someone shot by the Sikhs,' Isa related his experience of the morning.

'Think of it! They wanted to move a family, so some-one had to be killed. All through a misunderstanding. Dead for nothing.'

'Why did it have to happen like that?' commented Saleh after hearing Isa's story.

Isa shrugged his shoulders and his fingers plucked the strings of his violin.

'Play again,' said Saleh. Isa picked up the violin, pressed his chin against it and played once again the Heroic Polonaise of Chopin. This, too, is empty sound, thought Isa to himself; I'm only a fourth-rate player, I cannot put life and spirit into this music. He felt des-pondent for a moment, reflecting that neither as a hus-band was he a success. I have never been a success in my life—whether as a teacher or a husband or a violin-ist. He looked at Saleh who was absorbed listening. It's better to be like Saleh, he thought, not to think about things too deeply—not to feel with the heart and the mind too keenly. Take life as it comes. Don't ask ques-tions. Work like a machine. Morning enter the class, open the lesson book, begin to teach. Give marks. Punish the children who are naughty. Eat, sleep. Read the paper. Don't get irritated or frustrated reading reports or articles in the paper, and at night sleep with your wife or another woman. Sunday, take your child on your knee, sit on the verandah. Gossip over the fence with a neighbour, about some other neighbour.

He felt the melody he was playing grow progressively lifeless but he carried on. Until it was finished. He heard Selah clapping.

'What piece was that?' Saleh asked.

'Chopin. I can't play it well.'

'Really? It was very good.'

'Ah, but the spirit in this music—the spirit which Chopin infused into it. A fire burning with the love for his country—powerful as the gust of a hurricane . . . I cannot recreate that in my playing.'

Isa placed his violin back on the table and, after re-sining his bow, he put it and the violin back into the case. He opened the cupboard intending to put it away but suddenly stopped—deciding to take it to play at home—and locked the cupboard again.

'Shall we just go home?' he asked Saleh. 'It looks as if no one else is coming in today, and no children are going to come now.'

Saleh nodded. Isa went to call the school janitor and told the old man to lock up the school again. Saleh went off on his bicycle.

Isa walked to the tram stop at Djalan Asam Lama close to Pasar Baru. The trams were running again. They always kept going. They stopped if there was a clash, and then started again. The outer walls were painted with slogans in English 'Freedom is the birth-right of every nation', 'NICA—No Indonesian Cares About'.

In the tram a few people looked contemptuously at his violin, as though asking who was mad enough to carry a violin in days of violence such as these. People should carry weapons, and here is a man with a violin! Even though not bearing arms themselves it was still easy to sneer at another on such occasions.

That night as they were about to go to bed, they were startled by the shouts of 'Watch out! Watch out!' disturbing the precinct, and the sound of the footsteps of a youth running past. They waited half-an-hour more, but nothing else happened. Several times his wife had urged him to go out to take part in security patrols with their neighbours, but Isa was too much of a coward to go out of the house into the darkness, armed only with a bamboo spear sharpened for him by one of his pupils.

'The people opposite are beginning to look down on you because you never go out when there's a raid,' his wife said to him.

Isa drew his knees to his chest and pretended not to hear what she was saying.

For a long time in the dark of their bedroom they remained thus. Isa called his wife softly, 'Fatima'.

His wife, who was not yet asleep, pretended not to hear.

Isa realised that she was not asleep but he didn't dare to say anything.

He did not know when he fell asleep. He dreamt of the shooting at Djalan Asam Lama again. It was as vivid as though he were watching it on a cinema screen. He saw himself walking, then heard the shouts 'Watch out! Watch out!' There was a burst of firing and then the Chinese covered in blood. Then he saw himself crouching next to the wounded Chinese who twisted his head and looked up. Isa screamed in his dream. It was his face on the body of the Chinese—his face covered in blood.

Isa awoke. He was soaked in sweat. He stole a glance at his wife. Fatima was still asleep. In the gloom of their room her well-formed breasts rose and fell regularly— her full sweet lips lightly closed. For a moment he thought of embracing her, but he checked himself. He was afraid she would reject him, as she usually did.

He got up and placed his denture in a glass on the

45

dressing table—three lower front teeth. He often forgot. And if he forgot, the following morning his mouth was sour and foul smelling.

Throughout the night he felt totally isolated, in a world of darkness. There was no-one to respond to the cry of his heart yearning for love.

Fatima slept on.

Outside, throughout the night, the rumble of firing broke out repeatedly until it was almost dawn.

And it was not until dawn that Isa fell asleep again.

3

'Play your violin. Even though your technique isn't fluent or accomplished, you have a certain vitality,' said Isa encouragingly to Hazil.

'Yes, I know,' said Hazil. 'There is so little chance to practice.'

'Try once again. Let your feelings carry you, rising and falling, with the music. Don't think about it. Plunge yourself into the spirit of it. You can' . . . Hazil played again. Isa looked somewhat disapprovingly at the cigarette stub still smoking and alight and which was beginning to char the wood at the edge of the table.

No matter how many times he told him, Hazil always forgot to put his lighted cigarette on the ashtray.

Fatima too had scolded him several times for allowing Hazil to do so. Hazil always apologised if reminded of his carelessness. But every time he took a cigarette, he forgot again. And Hazil never stopped smoking. As soon as one was finished he lit another. His nails and long, slender fingers were stained with nicotine. Isa looked at Hazil as he played the violin.

He recalled their meeting two months earlier—their first meeting. The day after the shooting at Gang Adjudan. The youths had met at Kebon Sireh and because he was the Deputy-Chairman of the People's Security Committee, he was called on to be present.

Actually, he did not enjoy this responsibility and was very reluctant to be present. He took no pleasure in discussing ways and means of patrolling the precinct at night or organising plans for defence and the like. The sight of these young people carrying revolvers made his heart shrink within him. But how could he refuse? If he refused he would be suspect and everyone in the precinct treat him as an enemy. Even worse, he might be accused of being an enemy spy with all its consequences. He was afraid. And that was why he was present. The meeting was in a house right in the centre of the precinct. It was held after the evening prayer. The area surrounding the house was patrolled by youths armed with machetes, and bamboo spears. They behaved as if they were expecting the enemy to attack any moment so that Isa became even more nervous as he went in.

He remembered little of the fervid meeting. Everyone swore to dare death and sacrifice his life for freedom. It was Hazil who spoke the most, putting forward all kinds of plans to collect weapons. And then how startled he had been when he was chosen as courier for weapons and letters within Djakarta city. The reason the youths gave was that, because he was a schoolteacher, no one would suspect him.

He tried feebly to refuse. But a moment later felt himself sinking before the urgings which came upon him from all sides.

Home from the meeting he told his wife:

'In fact I'm scared, Fatima,' he said. 'I've never before been in an organisation such as this. Dealing in weapons—when I don't even know how to use a revolver. But if I don't do it, you know what people will say.'

'There's nothing to be afraid of,' Fatima replied. 'Isn't everyone in it? And if you don't, let's hope no one takes it into his head we're spies. You know how easy it is for a throat to be cut for nothing whatever.'

Isa shook his head.

'I'm a teacher,' he said. 'Not a warmonger.'

From there on Hazil often came to their house and gradually during those two months a strange kind of friendship had developed between them.

Sometimes Isa tried to analyse the feelings that bound them together. Hazil was thin, full of blazing enthusiasm, a quality he totally lacked. Fortunately, during those two months, there was no call upon his courage to carry weapons from one area of Djakarta to another. The youths were still fond of caressing their weapons and not one of them felt disposed to hand over a revolver, cartridge or hand-grenade to Isa.

It was music from which their friendship grew. Hazil was a composer. He played several of his compositions to Isa. And Isa was intrigued. There was something in Hazil's music which housed a tremendous vitality but which was still constricted. It was as though Hazil himself had not found the key to release his energies from confinement.

'You must get it out,' he urged Hazil time after time.

49

And Hazil always replied that he was fettered, that there were many things holding him back.

'I am still bound to the world in which I was born and in which I grew up,' he exclaimed angrily. Angry at himself, angry at Isa for his persistent questioning.

'I am bound to the respect and obedience a child owes his father; to the conventions of a man living in society; to the trust and loyalties of friendship. I am still bound to a concern with what others feel and think about me.'

And Isa would reply that a man could be free without surrendering such values.

To which Hazil responded that all these had to be discarded and new ones created deriving from new human experience. Only by the liberation of the self from all the old oppressions could people usher in a new and vigorous freedom, he exclaimed.

And if Isa persisted in saying that for the sake of his music Hazil must have the courage if necessary to be responsible to himself alone by throwing aside everything he felt restrained him, Hazil would reply 'If I do that am I not sinning? Suppose that later I should have to betray a friend? Is music more important than loyalty to a friend or to the Revolution? Then Isa fell silent. He could not answer. For he felt that had he to face that, he would yield without a struggle. He would accept any kind of bondage and oppression as long as he could live in peace.

After a while a strange feeling developed in him towards Hazil. The yearnings he had for himself he yearned for Hazil to achieve. Without realising it, he began to feel that even if he was not destined to be an accomplished violinist he still hoped that Hazil would;

and if he was only to compose songs for the school children he wanted to see Hazil create a new music.

Several experiences he shared with Hazil increased his sense of unconscious devotion. On one occasion they were on their way back from school; they were walking, and he was carrying his violin in its case.

As they were about to turn into Laan Holle they saw some British soldiers searching all cars and pedestrians. All passers-by were ordered to line up one by one to be searched.

Hazil whispered to him, 'They're looking for weapons. Where's the violin case? Isa handed it over; and Hazil took a revolver from his trouser pocket, put it inside the case and carried it. Isa urged Hazil to find another way round. But all the intersections were guarded, and they had to pass through the check point at Laan Holle.

As they approached the check point Isa became more and more frightened. Yet Hazil showed no anxiety—rather he spoke all the more fluently, from time to time laughing at his own jokes. As their turn came, Isa felt his body trembling. He was terrified that the English and the Indian soldiers conducting the search would see his guilt written all over his face.

But they paid no attention to the violin case Hazil was carrying, and after their pockets had been frisked they were allowed to pass.

It was long before Guru Isa felt the chill that throbbed the length of his spine and buried itself in his stomach disappear, or his knees stopped quaking. But Hazil had long been telling amusing stories and winking at him.

But alongside the feelings of anxiety, fear and horror

which fused to disturb him, Isa felt a little pride in himself because he had played a part in an underground organisation. It was a tonic to his emotions to think that he was taking part in the Struggle. Sometimes he even had a sense of superiority as he thought of his wife remaining at home whereas he had a dangerous task in addition to being a teacher.

Hazil stopped playing the violin and gave him an odd look—'Listen to this,' he said. 'And say nothing until I have finished.'

As Hazil's slender hand drew the second stroke of the bow across the strings something began to throb within Isa—something buried within the depths of his heart. It was a strange melody, beginning with a high soaring note, which suddenly plunged to the bottom of the register. Isa felt as though he had been hurled skyward, and then flung sharply, viciously, downwards.

For Isa the outer world ceased to exist. It was as though something enveloped the room in which they were—something which insulated them from the outer world; only the two of them and the music—a music from the world which entered the inner recesses of the human heart, whence it returned to the world again.

Then Isa realised the music Hazil had created was the music that he had wished to create but which was beyond him—it was the suffering of his own soul. It was his own hopes which soared skywards only to be beaten down, then soared again only to be beaten down even more cruelly. It was his doubts, anxieties, fears, terrors and sorrows, his pining for happiness. The music was full of bitter weeping and struggle, interspersed with melodies of a profound undulating calm.

Isa was startled from his absorption when Hazil took

the violin from his chin and placed it on the table. The silence which rose in the room after the final note had fled back to the world could be cut with a knife. Isa felt he should fly, pursue the vanished music swallowed up by the world. He looked away from the open window as he heard Hazil say, 'How was it?'

Although Hazil affected unconcern, Isa saw within him all the emotions which were inexpressible while he played the violin. His face muscles were still tense. 'How was it?' Hazil repeated.

There was a sound of clapping from the door. Isa turned his head. Fatima was clapping and smiling at Hazil.

'Wonderful', she said, her eyes shining as she looked at Hazil. Hazil bowed, in the manner of a conductor acknowledging tumultuous applause from the audience in the Opera House.

In his fascination Isa did not notice the look that passed between Fatima and Hazil. It was only for a moment, because Fatima quickly withdrew from the doorway and stepped into the next room blushing.

Hazil looked at Isa. 'Well, how about it?' he pressed.

'Whatever can one say about such music,' replied Isa. 'Tremendous! Tremendous!' he added quickly. He stood in front of Hazil and asked him, 'When did you write it? You never told me,' as though complaining he had not been told.

'During these last few weeks,' replied Hazil. 'I didn't dare to tell you because I was afraid it wouldn't come off. Up till now I was still anxious in case I lacked the stamina to portray the human struggle in my music, the perennial human struggle, the struggle for happiness.'

'Did you feel it?' he asked Isa again.

'Yes, its all there. Have no doubt. I felt it, all of it, all of it.'

Hazil smiled to see Isa so enthusiastically attempting to convince him that his music was good.

'It is an orchestral piece', said Hazil, 'but there is no orchestra to play it.' In his voice there was a trace of sadness and regret.

'This music sings the struggle of man as man,' Hazil continued, his voice vibrant again. 'Man as an individual. Do you know what I mean? How can I explain it? The struggle of man, not as one of a herd; not the bark of jackals hunting in a pack but the bark, the growl, the pain and sharp cry of the individual jackal in his struggle for life. For me the individual is an end, and not the means to an end. Human happiness lies in a perfect and harmonious development of the individual with his fellows. The state is merely a means; the individual must not be subordinated to the State. This music is my life. This is the road with no end I must follow. This is the revolution we have begun. Revolution is only a means to attain freedom, and freedom is only a means to enrich the happiness and nobility of human life.'

As he spoke, Isa was conscious only of an emptiness in the words Hazil uttered. He felt he was merely reading a book. He himself had not the strength to bring forth such men. He preferred to yield to the shelter of the herd—the herd which swallowed up the human individual. There was much to be said for losing one's identity in the herd. There is no longer responsibility— the sense of duty can be safely buried and among the masses one can find a secure hiding place. In the absence of a personality a kind of shelter—shield—a

protection against others. But Isa did not dare to express these thoughts.

'How can a free man live shackled as one of a herd?' insisted Hazil. 'Indonesian man as a herd has been oppressed by the Dutch for more than three hundred and fifty years. Such are the masses; in themselves they are meaningless. The herd itself can only move because there are individuals who can raise themselves above it. And my music is not that of the herd but of the individual human beings who comprise it.

Isa wished that he could speak with this confidence. But he was afraid that Hazil would think his feelings worthless, and so he spoke only of music.

'Have you thought of your music played by an orchestra and the role of a drum in such an orchestra—a great Indonesian music must have a drum—this has always been the case, I think', said Isa, 'because the drum has existed in the Indonesian world from ancient times. Just think! The drum beaten at a marriage—the drum at the celebration of a birth—at all State festivals; the drum calling people to prayer—the drum when people march out to war.'

'Yes,' said Hazil. He turned to the window and looked at the sky outside, his voice as it were coming from afar off.

'You are right. The role of the drum in Indonesian music has never been studied. My music, performed by an orchestra, with the vivid use of the drum which can be used to express loneliness, fear, joy and teror.' Hazil clenched his fingers and approached Isa.

'You are a genius,' he said slapping Isa on the shoulder, 'You have given me a new idea.' 'Hah!' he exclaimed. 'Who says that Indonesian music

55

does not have hidden resources on which to draw?'

Fatima entered with the tea.

'Your music is wonderful', she said to Hazil, setting the tea on the table next to where he was standing.

'Thank you, but it's only an attempt,' said Hazil.

'No, not an attempt—a full creation,' cried Isa.

'You and I, the pair of us, will make a magnificent concert piece from this melody', said Hazil inviting Isa.

Isa was delighted to hear Hazil's invitation.

'Yes. Yes', he said. 'Perhaps we can do it'.

'Of course we can', said Hazil joyfully and full of enthusiasm. 'We'll start work right now.'

'But do you realise the difficulty', Isa asked Hazil, 'of writing music for the drum?'

Hazil fell silent for a moment, seeing the point. They were both silent. Fatima had left the room again.

'Perhaps there's a simple solution', said Isa after a moment. 'We need the drum to create the rhythmic pattern that will produce the atmosphere we want; then we can gradually fade it until it is just a background to the music'.

Hazil sipped his tea. And Isa once again felt somewhat irritated to see Hazil throwing his cigarette ash carelessly onto the floor.

'How are you getting on with your father now?' asked Isa.

'Oh, my father', answered Hazil. 'Yesterday he was still angry with me because we came back late from the meeting. Sometimes he does not say a word and pays no attention to my activities; and there are times when he is furiously angry because I support the revolution. It's always the same insults. We're just murderers and plunderers, neither more nor less. 'It's a pity he's my father, otherwise he would have been kidnapped,' Hazil continued embittered. 'I don't understand how the old man's mind works!'

'Perhaps he, too, is uncertain of himself', said Isa. 'In times like these many people are confused—they don't know what to do. Self interest and national interest are at odds. They are frightened, subject to all kinds of pressures, victims of all kinds of threats'—he was telling himself his own feelings, although Hazil didn't know it.

'In the struggle for Freedom there is no room for doubt or confusion,' said Hazil. 'From the beginning I have never had any doubt. I have always known, from the very beginning, that the road we have taken is a road with no end. And we are to follow it without wavering, from this point onwards, onwards, onwards; there is no end. Even when we have Freedom we have not reached the end. Where is the end of the road of struggle in pursuit of human happiness? In human life there are always enemies and difficulties to be faced and overcome—After one, another appears, and then another. Once we have chosen the path of struggle, we have set foot on a road with no end; and you, I, all of us have chosen the path of struggle.'

Isa had no ready answer. On hearing Hazil's words, he saw in his mind's eye a road with no end—a road stretching before his eyes, on and on, into the limitless distance, without an end; beginning in darkness, disappearing and continuing into darkness. A road that was no more than a streak of lightning in a dark world, sharply defined and fearsome. The road with no end which awoke such enthusiasm in Hazil was to Isa a terrifying nightmare that made sleep a thing of terror.

E

Mr. Kamarudin had been ill for a few days, and had not left his room. For a week now Hazil had not come home at all. He had been to Krawang and Bekasi to attend to the lines of communication between the peoples' volunteers in the Greater Djakarta area outside the city with those within the city. Kamarudin was pining for Hazil. A pining mixed with regret that when Hazil, about to set out, had asked him for money for expenses, he had scolded him and shouted that if he wished to fight for Freedom he should do so on his own account. Now that he was ill in bed all kinds of thoughts such as he rarely dwelt on came into his mind.

He regretted his frequent recent quarrels with Hazil. Now there are only the two of us left, thought Kamarudin. His mother is dead and I should take her place. In times such as these father and son must help each other. But why would not Hazil obey him any more? Under Dutch rule and during the Japanese occupation Hazil had always been a well-behaved child. He had always listened to his father; but now how much he had changed! Kamarudin felt that Hazil had become rough and wild during this period of revolution. What will become of him later? he thought sadly.

Then he thought of himself. He had tried quietly to get into touch with the Dutch and made tactful enquiries as to whether they would employ him again. They had made him certain promises but also indicated that for a person as old as he, now over sixty, there was no suitable opening. They had also indicated, however, that if he had influence and prestige among the people at large the situation might change radically. This was what made Mr. Kamarudin so angry. He knew that he had been a good official. He had done his utmost to administer every regulation and instruction. But only that. He had never before taken part in political life under the old regime, and his name was completely unknown. He had been merely a good cog in the colonial machine. But now a new kind of cog was needed, which could be used to cheat the people. The Dutch wanted people who could be regarded as leaders trusted by the people through whom they could carry out their designs.

And so the Dutch had no use for Mr. Kamarudin who was old, and had no influence whatever. 'We will pay your pension, and if a suitable position becomes available we will get into touch with you.' Mr. Kamarudin was very confused. After coming back from his interview with the Dutch he felt discontented. He lost his appetite. He felt a complete stranger to the world about him. He had nothing in common with the youths who shouted 'Watch out' and 'Merdeka'. And those with whom he thought he could work, and enjoy a comfortable life as he had before, did not welcome him with open arms. At first he had thought that the Dutch would be glad to employ him again. He knew several of his friends who had received definite undertakings from the Dutch when the time came. But when he considered the matter further he realised that their positions were not similar. One was of feudal descent and had considerable influence among the rural families of the Southern Celebes; the other was credited with considerable influence among the aristocracy of West Java. I am only an old man without influence whose usefulness is finished, thought Mr. Kamarudin bitterly.

At that moment he very much wished Hazil had come back from Krawang. In the youth of his son he wanted to recapture the vitality he had once known. Mr. Kamarudin looked at the table at the end of the room. A photograph of his wife who had died during the Japanese occupation was facing the bed.

His grief deepened. He remembered when Hazil was born. That was twenty-five years ago. Then he was still a Judge in Kalimantan. It had been a good life, Kamarudin recalled. You only had to work and after office hours return to your wife and your child. And he remembered his affairs with other women; secret affairs. I certainly enjoyed them, Kamarudin thought with a touch of satisfaction as his thoughts revolved around himself. Only once, no—twice, his wife had found him out and then there had been a row. Kamarudin smiled to himself as he thought of it. Why did I forget to take her handkerchief out of my pocket? he mused. And on the other occasion it had been the woman's fault—she had told someone else.

Then Kamarudin thought of Hazil and his bewilderment deepened. I don't understand the youth of today. They are all mad, mad. They respect nothing, they're filled with their own ideas.

But I'll make it up with Hazil when he returns, thought Kamarudin. He must come home and not carry on in this mad way. I'll talk to him once he has come home, thought Kamarudin.

And the house was silent. There was no sound of life. It was the house of an old man; the young folk had deserted it to build a new house of their own.

4

It drizzled that night, with an occasional heavy shower
followed by drizzle again. The houses were all shut up
and the doors had been barred since sunset. In these
days fraught with danger and menace, even flimsy
bamboo walls and a door which could be locked or
barred gave a feeling of security and shelter. Fatima
was lying on the bed and Isa working in his study. The
light from a 40 watt lamp was hardly sufficient for the
room. He was waiting for Hazil who had told him he
was coming that night on an important matter related
to the Struggle. Hazil had returned from Krawang and
Bekasi. The message was that he would be there at
eight o'clock but Isa looked at the alarm clock on the
table—it was already almost ten and Hazil had still not
come.

The door between the bedroom and the study was
open. If Isa looked through the doorway he could see his

wife's feet and her well-formed calves up to a little below the knee. Beneath her was the embroidered sheet reaching almost to the floor. Besides that—besides his wife and the bedroom, there was something on Isa's mind. Besides his wife, there was still something in his memory. He still knew . . . his thoughts returned to the first, second, the third night of their marriage.

He drew a deep breath, got up and went to the window and lifted up the margarine tin which was full of water. He had placed it there since the rain started to catch the water dripping from the ceiling. He opened the window a little and the wind blew the cold spray against his face. Isa shivered for a moment at the touch of the cold, dank hand of night, like the hand of Death caressing his face. Quickly he emptied out the water and closed the window.

He put the margarine tin back on the floor and sat again at the table. He felt even more anxious. A rainy night such as this was the time for violence to be wrought against human beings. He could not concentrate enough to mark the pupils' work. Now the noise of the rain on the roof was drowned out by the sound of the water dripping into the tin; it drowned out even the ticking of the alarm clock on the table. Isa wanted to throw out the tin so that the sound of dripping would cease, but he was afraid that the wet floor would make his wife angry with him the next day.

Isa looked again at the alarm clock. It was almost ten thirty. He shut the exercise book he was marking and placed it on the pile of books he had finished. He ran his fingers through his hair and rested his forehead on his hands on the table. He longed for his wife to come to him, or to go to her and then to sleep in close embrace on the cold night with the rain beating down, to bury every anxiety and uncertainty in a full and warm embrace. And not to think, not to think—not to remember, not to remember.

Isa took a deep breath. He knew it was not possible. It could never be until something changed.

Isa felt weary, leaned his head back against the chair, and without realising it fell asleep.

The rain fell harder and the sound of the water dripping in the margarine tin lessened as it filled. Isa dreamt he was walking alone on a broad, smooth road. It was a straight road, and from the spot where he was walking it extended without a break to a pitch-dark and threatening horizon. Hazil was shouting behind him: 'Hurry, hurry, I'll soon be with you.'

And Isa was walking. At first he felt uncomfortable walking alone; but on either side of the road were shady trees and beautiful flowers such as he had never seen before. He looked back from time to time, seeking Hazil but Hazil had not come into sight. And when he looked ahead again it seemed that the road had changed. There were no longer any leafy trees or beautiful flowers; and the sun had become a red ball in a jet-black sky.

Isa felt unbearably hot, his chest was constricted and he could hardly breathe the air heavy as lead. He turned and started to run back; but the road that he had traversed had disappeared and there remained only the road straight ahead—straight and lonely, disappearing in the dark of the horizon. It was terrifying. Isa ran with all his might. He no longer knew from where he came. He ran only to get to the end of the road as soon as possible. But the road had no end. And as fast as Isa ran, so fast did the road recede into the pitch black horizon.

As he was running, a fast-driven jeep suddenly overtook him, and he caught a glimpse of Fatima and Hazil inside it. They didn't even glance at him. He tried to call them, but from his heaving constricted chest came only a hoarse croak. He collapsed onto the road, and in despair wept.

The pitch black sky descended upon him; he was in a confined space, and the sun, like a ball of blazing fire, was rushing down as though to crush him.

Terror-stricken, he watched it coming towards him like a bullet. His eyes were blinded and he screamed as it exploded on him with a roar like thunder . . . he was awake . . . His wife was shaking him and asking: 'Isa, what is the matter with you?'

Isa pushed his wife's hand aside roughly; he stood up and then remembered . . . he was conscious and awake. He smiled weakly, embarrassed and said, 'Sorry, I had a nightmare.' He wiped with his hand the heavy sweat on his forehead and temples. He looked at his wife and she looked at him. He was looking for something in her eyes—a light or a radiance he had long been seeking but never found. It was the light that had been there before their marriage and for a few months afterwards— that light of love and affection which had long vanished from her dark bright eyes. To Isa it seemed that he had waited for a long time for this light to be rekindled. He knew it would not return now any more than it had on past occasions; yet he still hoped.

It was hard for him to turn away his eyes; to the last moment he was still hoping. As on the other occasions he was overwhelmed with sorrow—it filled him with loathing and misery to see Fatima's eyes devoid of love and affection. They were the eyes of a stranger feeling pity for a fellow human being. Perhaps there was something of friendship—only that—nothing more—nothing deeper or more intimate.

Isa feared her love for him had vanished for ever. 'I'll get you a glass of cold tea,' said Fatima, in a calm and pleasant voice. But the tone was that which she used when she was comforting Salim if he cried or was frightened.

Fatima left the room and Isa sat down again.

'I must settle this. I must have a decision,' he said urging himself. He wanted a confrontation with Fatima. He could no longer live like this. Either Fatima loved him and would help him, or she must go. But in his heart he feared that he had not the courage to face or accept the decision she would take. He was afraid, and knew full well how Fatima would decide if he forced her to a showdown. 'But I must discuss it,' Isa urged to himself.

He wracked his brains seeking a way to begin such a discussion with Fatima. What should he say? He heard her footsteps approaching. Perspiration glistened again on his forehead. He felt in dire straits because he still did not know what to say. He had decided that the best moment would be as Fatima handed the glass to him and he took her hand while taking it. That was the moment to broach the subject. But he still did not know what to say. Her steps drew closer. Isa was at his wits' end. He still did not know what to say, no matter how hard he tried.

At last it was Fatima who put an end to his confusion. She came in and gave him the glass. He was so moved that he took it with a trembling hand; then she stroked his hair and rubbed his brow with her cool and smooth hand.

Isa quickly put the glass on the table, took her hand and said, 'Fatima', putting into the word all his feelings, hopes, dreams and fears, the whole of his heart longing for love.

She apparently understood and remained silent and motionless. Isa did not dare to look at or seek her eyes. He was afraid. He pushed aside the fear. What had happened earlier as he had awakened from his dream would happen again now. He could feel it. Now it had happened. But, as always, he was still hoping even though his hope was haunted with fear, and he knew that what he was waiting for could not come.

'Fatima', he said again, and this time without his intending it there was an urgency in his tone.

She felt it too. She withdrew her hand and spoke to him gently: 'Do we have to go through all that again?'

Isa remained silent. Fatima went back to the bedroom and said, 'Sleep now, Isa. Perhaps he won't come now because of the rain.' Isa did not answer. The sound of water dripping into the margarine tin seemed to be jeering at him. He sat gazing at the embroidery on the white sheet.

Fatima lay on the bed, unable to get back to sleep. The event in the next room reminded her again of the quarrel a few days after the disastrous night, six months after their marriage; and then their attempts together or Isa's alone which were always unsuccessful. All kinds of feelings rose in her heart; disappointment, frustration, anger, sorrow and embarrassment—embarrassment at herself and at her husband.

At length everything had come to a head and exploded one night, after which they decided not to try again.

'What is there left of our marriage then?' Isa had asked that night.

She replied 'I will be a good wife to you. Just that.'

'Without love?' pressed Isa. 'Without love,' she replied. The words were born of frustration; but having said them, she could not go back on them.

And from then on they grew further apart. Isa lived with his own thoughts and dreams, despairs and hopes, and his own self.

Fatima was never unfaithful to him. Perhaps indeed, a woman is more able to control herself than a man in such a situation—or perhaps her upbringing served to restrain her. Certainly it was not religion which kept her from seeking satisfaction outside the house; she herself never prayed—neither did Isa. But there was something in sexual relationships apart from her husband which filled her with loathing. She felt disgust at the thought of herself handled by a man to whom she was not married.

Across her dreams there sometimes fell the image of a man. But that was different. Yet recently her thoughts had been troubled by the form of a man—clear and definite. His face was thin and sharp—his nose elevated and thin—his eyes flaming and bloodshot—and his music excited her. Hazil. The image of Hazil very frequently entered her thoughts, so that she became doubtful of herself. She did not want to be troubled by such images because she regarded herself as a woman of good upbringing, respectable, educated and of healthy mind.

When these imaginings pursued her she longed to find shelter in Isa's embrace—and if at this moment,

67

this very moment, Isa had come and roughly and violently seized her, and kissed her and forced her to make love to him she would have rejoiced, yielded willingly and responded to him. Although she did not realise it, she was a woman whose body and soul longed to be seized and mastered.

When Isa came to bed, Fatima lay still, pretending to be asleep. From the stiffness of her posture Isa could see that she was not asleep. 'Fatima', he whispered, but Fatima remained taut, still pretending to be asleep.

Isa sighed and quietly lay down beside his wife. Outside, the rain poured down steadily, interspersed by a succession of gusts of wind as though a giant hand gave an occasional wave of a fan.

Just as he fell asleep, Isa awoke with a start as he heard a loud crack like a shot. A rotten bough of the jackfruit tree broken off by the wind had fallen on the zinc roof of the house next door.

Isa fell asleep again pursued by all kinds of nightmares.

The echoing rifle fire throughout the city did not subside that night.

5

The next morning Isa woke early. He had not slept well; his mouth felt sour and his head was heavy and aching. Outside it was still drizzling. Fatima was already up and he could hear her singing to herself in the kitchen.

He went to his study. He felt disgusted at the sight of the wet floor where the rainwater had overflowed from the margarine tin. He opened the window and threw out the water.

The cry of a startled child beneath the window made him jump. He glanced out. Little Salim looked up at him accusingly. He had been soused with the water. Isa was startled and then filled with regret. For a moment he was afraid in case Salim was angry with him. The adult and the child gazed at each other for a moment. Slowly a smile formed on Salim's lips and he cried out, 'Come on, do it again!'

Isa laughed and said, 'There's no more water,' and he showed Salim the empty tin. Then he said, 'Come inside at once. Don't play in the drizzle. You'll get a chill. We'll bathe together.'

In the bathroom he played with little Salim. He felt gay again and the cold water dispelled his headache. He put on his clothes while singing to himself.

Over breakfast his gaiety ebbed. On the table there was only black coffee without sugar and a few pieces of boiled cassava, warmed up leftovers from the night before.

'If you don't get any money today I don't know where I can get rice on credit,' said Fatima passing him the coffee. 'There's no sugar left. I owe Bibi Tatang five litres of rice. I still haven't paid it back although I promised her within two days. It's difficult even to get vegetables at the store now. And for a long time I haven't been able to pay the greengrocer.'

Isa didn't answer. He drank the bitter, hot coffee which scalded his tongue and his throat and warmed his stomach. He did not blame Fatima. His salary was no longer enough for them to eat, particularly now that payments were only made irregularly and sometimes they only received what was called 'assistance'.

He looked at the table and thought to himself. Actually, to live contentedly they needed very little. Two litres of rice a day, a little meat and vegetables, a little sugar for coffee and once a month a kebaja* for Fatima, a suit for Salim and a shirt or pair of trousers for himself.

But there had been none of this now for a long time.

'I'll try to get an advance at school, Fatima,' he said,

*Indonesian style blouse.

draining his cup. He got up and went to get his brief-case. The rain had stopped and the day was bright and clear.

'Good-morning!' said Hamidy the next door neigh-bour, greeting him.

Isa looked at him. Hamidy was short and stout. During the Japanese occupation he had had no fixed occupation but was never without money. He was a merchant or a black marketeer. Isa didn't like him. He had heard many stories about him in the precinct. Now rumour had it he dealt in rice. He was said to be very stingy. But Isa had also heard that now he made large contributions to the Revolution, funds for the night-watch and the like.

'Good morning, Mr. Hamidy' he said returning a friendly smile. And he stopped. 'How is the rice from Krawang now?' he asked. An idea had come into his head.

'This week not a sack has come in. Everything has been held up by the Youth at Tjikarang.' The thought which had entered Isa's head departed again.

'We want to borrow your truck for a while this after-noon', said Isa, remembering Hazil's letter asking him to try to find transport, 'For the Revolution, to carry . . . you know what.'

'Simple, simple. What time do you need it? I'll have it ready,' Hamidy replied. 'In the Revolution we must all help each other mustn't we? When the rice comes through I want to contribute a sack or two.'

'Many thanks. We'll be needing it at about three o'clock,' said Isa.

'O.K. O.K.' said Hamidy.

Isa continued on his way to the tram stop at the end

of Gang Djaksa in Djalan Asam Lama. Near the inter-section of his alley Pak Damrah greeted him 'Merdeka' as he passed. Baba Tan who was standing in front of his stall shouted 'Good morning, Teacher.' Every morning as he passed these two people always greeted him thus.

The tram left just as he reached the end of the road and Isa had to wait for the next one. He felt irritated and thought, if I hadn't stopped to speak with Hamidy I wouldn't have missed it.

Isa taught mechanically. His thoughts were not on the lesson. He wanted school to be quickly over; he wanted to meet Hazil as soon as possible, he wanted to hear what Hazil had to say and perhaps have some music with him. Hazil had brought a drum and when they practised Hazil's piece they played the instruments in turn. While they played Isa was able to taste hap-piness and forgot his fears and anxiety.

The recess came, and this was the best time to ask for an advance of salary. But Isa was anxious and felt doubtful. He was afraid he would feel embarrassed if the Headmaster rejected his request. At the same time his gloom increased as he reflected that if he did not bring home money, Fatima would berate him. Eventu-ally after debating for a long time with himself, he decided to ask. But, just at that moment, the bell went and he had to return to class. The opportunity had gone.

School was over, but Isa felt relieved that he had been saved by the bell from the need to ask. He hated to ask this way. He felt as though he were having to beg. If the request was granted it would not be so bad, but if it were rejected then the shame would embarrass him for days afterwards.

Isa still had not gone home. He felt loath to face Fatima. He sat at his desk marking the pupils' work. At last the exercise books were finished. He got up and went to the cupboard to put away the books he had corrected. As he was about to shut it again his eyes fell upon a package of new exercise books. Something flashed through his mind—something which said that by taking and selling a few dozen of them he could get some money.

He checked himself and had a moment of inner struggle. Suddenly he felt ashamed that his own thoughts should suggest that he steal.

How could I sink so low as to steal from my own school, he thought bitterly and shamefully. He felt as though a whol e crowd was looking at him, watching the thoughts in his head, reading there his desire to steal.

No one would know if I took ten or fifteen. Who checks them now? said the thoughts urging him to steal.

They'll sell easily at the Chinese shop at Tanah Abang for seven-and-a-half rupiah each. Ten would bring seventy-five rupiah. That would be something.

Isa looked around. He looked to the door. He pinned his ears for the sound of footsteps. The school was silent, but it seemed he heard outside the school dozens of silent footsteps of spectators peeping at what he was doing. His heart trembled. His blood pounded against his skull. His breath became rapid. A cold sweat broke out on his back, temples, and the palms of his hands.

His mouth felt dry and with a trembling hand Isa opened the package of new exercise books. He took ten and then shut the cupboard again.

Quickly and hurriedly he put them into his briefcase. Only when he had shut it did he feel a little easier and his breath return to normal. He took a glass and went out to the tap. He drank a glass of cold water to calm himself.

As he left the school building, walking to Tanah Abang he continually accused himself. I have stolen. I'm a thief. I'm a thief. He scourged and tortured himself mercilessly, stripping and searing his spirit. As though he found satisfaction in torturing himself in this way; as though he felt that this self-torture served as retribution for the sin of theft he had committed. As though for the theft restitution were still possible.

Isa had not the courage to protest or bargain when the Chinese owner of the shop offered him only five rupiah each for the exercise books. He knew well enough that he could have got a better price had he been firm. But he had lost the will and the courage to be firm.

The fifty rupiah from the sale of the books weighed heavily in his pocket, and pressed hot against his body; he felt everyone who saw him knew his terrible secret.

He reached home feeling listless. He had a headache and his temples were pounding.

'I could only get fifty rupiah, Fatima,' he said, handing over the money as he told the lie. This was the first lie he had ever told in the whole of their married life, and he felt it even more bitterly than his theft of the books. But there was consolation at the expression of relief appearing on Fatima's face, the disappearance of the tenseness which anxiety about the following day's meal always brought.

'At least for a few days I don't have to worry about my house-keeping', said Fatima gaily.

'Hasn't Hazil come yet?' he asked her as they were sitting at the table.

'Not yet.'

'Where's Salim?'

'He ate first. He's gone out to play now. Were you able to borrow the truck from Hamidy next door?'

'Yes, but he's a rogue. He pretends to be helping us. Goodness knows how much he's made bringing rice from Krawang to Djakarta. And he's going to give us a sack or two, so he says—all talk.'

'You don't like him?'

'No. I don't like phoneys.'

He fell silent after saying this realising that now he too was a phoney. It had never occurred to Isa that there was no one in the world who did not indulge in pretence at some time or other. People did it for many reasons. Some to hide their fear, some to hide their sorrow, some to hide their joy, some their pride. One wanted to conceal falsehood, another truth—to conceal love, hate, and a thousand and one other things, and pretence served them all.

Isa felt unable to say anything more. Fatima looked at him rather strangely.

'Why are you suddenly quiet?' she asked.

'O, nothing'.

'Perhaps you're thinking of the job this afternoon.'

'On no. That's easy.' There, I'm putting up a pretence again, he thought as he was saying it. In fact since the night before and during the whole course of the morning's work what they were to do that afternoon had been at the back of his mind, knocking, requesting admission; requesting admission so that his mind could dwell on it. Now it had entered and filled his thoughts. Hazil's plan to transport four cases of ammunition and hand grenades of Japanese and American manufacture terrified him. The Japanese ones had been obtained from Japanese soldiers, the American ones bought from Indian Muslim soldiers.

If we move them in broad daylight, none of the British troops will suspect that we are carrying munitions, wrote Hazil in his letter; so do what you can to borrow Hamidy's truck from next door.

The goods were stored at Asam Reges and had to be taken to Manggarai. At Manggarai they were to be hidden in the house of a friend, and smuggled in small lots to Krawang by train.

Isa actually did not want to take part. This was the first time since he had joined the Organisation that he had been asked to carry arms. They are the experts at warfare, not me, thought Isa.

'What are you thinking about?' Fatima's question startled him.

'I am thinking its hardly right for me to go along with these hot blooded youths,' said Isa.

'Yes, but they need you,' replied Fatima. 'They're only children.'

Isa laughed to himself—laughed at himself and at Fatima. Fatima is extraordinarily naïve, he thought, if she still thinks and believes that I can lead these 'children' in revolt. And he suspected that she was making fun of him.

There was no one who could lead them—not even from among themselves. For a moment everything seemed clear to Isa. It was as though he could hold the problem in his fingertips and explain it to Fatima.

'In the Revolution'—he put his thoughts together 'Many people have to play a part which is alien to them.' Now his own position became clearer to him.

'You see, I am a teacher. I do not like violence. I

have never been one for quarrels. I hate fighting. I regret quarrelling as something coarse and uncivilised. But they have chosen me as a leader in the Struggle. I do not like this role. But I accept it. Do you know why I accept it? Not because I am embued with a flaming spirit of revolt or because I have a passionate love for my country. I love my country but there is not, or not yet, in my blood any trace of emotion urging me to sacrifice my life or shed my blood for it. I have never lived in a country to be redeemed by blood; and if there's anyone who claims to possess this spirit, then it is something false and contrived. I accept this role because I am afraid, and I am even more fearful, having accepted it, because I must do things I am afraid to do.' He looked at Fatima expectantly. Fatima would sneer at him and say he was a coward.

But Fatima was silent, and was looking at him attentively.

'I only want to know whether there are others like me,' Isa asked of no one in particular. But he did not dare to continue. Fatima looked at him.

'Do eat. I admire a man with the courage to transport weapons,' she said suddenly.

Isa felt relieved. He almost felt he was in the clouds. He ate again. Such moments of mutual understanding were few and thus very precious to him.

Hazil did not arrive until almost four o'clock. He at once apologised.

'I'm sorry I couldn't make it last night. I was held up at Sawah Besar. The rain was very heavy. Did you get the truck?'

'It's fixed,' said Isa. Hazil declined to sit and drink the tea Fatima was proffering.

'We'll be late. They're waiting. Come along, quickly,' he said to Isa. Isa was a little regretful that there was no time for some music first, but he concealed his disappointment and hurried after Hazil who was waiting in the alley in front of the house.

'Just a moment,' said Isa. 'You wait here. I'll ask where the truck is.' He scuttled into Hamidy's yard. The door was shut. He knocked. A moment later Hamidy came out wearing a sarong and a vest. Sweat was trickling from the nape of his neck down onto his chest and his fleshy back.

'Merdeka!' he exclaimed. 'O, Isa,' he went on respectfully, 'sorry I am not dressed. It's very hot this afternoon.'

'I came to ask where the truck is,' said Isa.

'O, I've arranged it. It's at Kebon Sireh Wetan in front of the "Modern Tailor". The driver's there.'

'Thanks. We're in a hurry. Merdeka.'

'Merdeka.' Hamidy closed the door and hurried back to his bedroom. His wife was lying in bed waiting for him. Hamidy quickly shut the door behind him.

Hamidy's truck was a patchwork affair. Its pedigree was lost forever. It had been a Chevrolet but all kinds of spare parts had been fitted so that it could still go. Traces of Japanese characters scraped off the side of it were still visible and Isa could distinguish the word Kaigun* on the hood.

It was a very old Chevrolet. Its headlights were like empty eye-sockets, and the step up was fastened onto the body with wire. Both mudguards were eroded with rust. The youths climbed onto it like monkeys leaping about on trees.

*Navy.

'Can it go?' shouted Hazil, kicking the back tyre.

The driver who was sitting talking with the seam-stresses saw them coming and came out and shouted 'Merdeka'. He knew Isa.

'Tell him where we are to go,' said Isa.

'What's your name?' asked Hazil.

'Abdullah.'

'Abdullah, will this truck go?' asked Hazil.

Abdullah laughed and said. 'It's in a bad way, but it's mobile'. He got up and sat behind the wheel and pressed the starter. The starting motor turned for a moment and then went dead. Adbullah tried it again. It turned once more then went dead again.

'How can it go?' Hazil accused.

Abdullah said, 'It's a brute. This morning it went perfectly. But it does have a shaky starter.'

The youths clambering on the truck shouted, 'Push, push.'

And so the truck was pushed. The seamstresses came out leaving their work to help. Two betja drivers standing drinking coffee joined in. So did the owner of the coffee stall.

After twenty metres the engine began to turn over, coughed and then fired—like the thunder of an old ship's engine. The youths yelled with enthusiasm and jumped in asking to take it around. Abdullah was angry and ordered them out.

'Do you think this is a game? This is for the Revolution. All of you, get out!'

Screaming and shouting, 'Merdeka. Merdeka', the youths leapt like wild monkeys down onto the road. Isa and Hazil got into the cabin and sat beside Abdul-lah.

'Everyone's glad to help the Revolution,' said Abdullah gaily. 'Where are we going?'

'To Asam Reges, in front of the lemonade factory,' replied Hazil.

The three of them were silent for a moment, then Hazil said to Abdullah, 'Do you know what we are going to carry?'

Abdullah grinned, showing his big dirty yellow teeth. He spat onto the road, and thumped his hand onto the wheel and said:

'Carry what you like, I'm with you.'

'This can be dangerous,' said Hazil. 'We're going to pick up weapons and take them to Manggarai. There we are going to hide them then smuggle them to Krawang. Are you still with us?'

Abdullah replied, 'If you and the teacher dare, why shouldn't I?'

On hearing this Isa said to himself, 'I don't dare, so why should I have to take part?'

'I've had some brushes with their soldiers.' Abdullah said. 'The Muslim Indians are good to us. It's the Gurkhas who are fierce. But when are we going to lay into all these whites, the English, the Americans and the Dutch?'

'We are not fighting the English and the Americans. Only the Dutch are our enemies,' said Hazil.

'Don't you believe it. Hasn't Bung Karno said we must starch the English and iron the Americans. Ordinary folk only follow their leaders. If they're told to go to the left, they go to the left—to the right, they go to the right. Naturally we know nothing of politics. There's only one thing I don't understand. Why haven't we started yet? The villagers are full of spirit. Everywhere the people are ready.'

'If you want to fight, Djakarta's no longer the place for it,' said Hazil. 'We can't fight here. The enemy is too strong. Therefore we must make preparations outside the city. That's why these weapons must be taken out of town.'

'That's all out of my depth', said Abdullah.

The engine stalled again near Petjenongon, but it was easy to get help. There were passers-by to give them a push and soon they had arrived in front of the lemonade factory.

'Back round to the back of the factory' said Hazil to the driver; and wait there.'

He and Isa jumped down. They followed a muddy, winding alley until Isa lost all sense of direction. Then Hazil stopped in front of a shack, knocked on the door and went in.

'Merdeka, Rachmat, the truck's on the road,' he shouted from outside.

The door opened slowly, and a nose, an eye, a forehead and a tuft of hair surveyed them from behind the door. When the eye recognised Hazil, the door opened wide and a voice greeted him: 'Merdeka. You're very late. We thought you weren't coming.'

'This is Isa, our friend,' said Hazil, introducing Isa. 'This is Rachmat of the People's Forces at Bekasi.'

Isa and Rachmat shook hands. When they entered, Isa saw three others in the murky darkness of the hovel. Hazil apparently knew all of them. He greeted them with 'Merdeka' and then sat on a trestle near them. Isa stepped forward and introduced himself. As his eyes grew accustomed to the gloom, he felt somewhat uncomfortable.

Si Ontong who sat to the left of Hazil was precisely

as Isa would have envisaged a lout of Senin.* His face was coarse and almost square, his eyebrows narrow and his hair straight and coarse as roof fibre. His lips were thick and protruding, his eyes fiery and bloodshot. He was wearing only coarse black cotton shorts and an old striped sailor shirt. The flesh of his huge fat thighs was thick with grime and filth, A red kerchief was bound around his head, and at his waist was a machete.

Isa felt he was face to face with something ferocious, nakedly primitive and with an unrestrainable passion for cruelty. The other two were no more prepossessing in appearance than Ontong: Kiran and Imam.

'O.K?' said Hazil to Rachmat.

Now Isa could see Rachmat more clearly. He was about the same age as Hazil. The thought flashed through his mind: these revolutionaries are very young. Some of them struggle realising what has been entrusted to them, but others treat it as a game—a search for excitement.

As yet there was no trace on Hazil of the hard lines and cruel wrinkles around the mouth visible on the countenances of these youths who had been fighting for several months—lines reflecting their knowledge of blood, murder, rapine, cruelty and sacrifice which before had been quite alien to them.

The lines around Rachmat's mouth were growing tense and hard. Isa felt he was looking at innocence violated, as though Rachmat had had some awesome experience—something neither sought nor asked for, which had been forced upon him.

'O.K.' said Rachmat to the three others in response to Hazil's call to get moving. They got up and went to the

*A well-known area of Djakarta.

back of the shack. Behind it there was a coconut plantation overgrown with scrub. About twenty metres from
their meeting place there was another hovel where
firewood and newly picked coconuts were stored. Beside
it was an old well. Its bricks were covered with dark
green moss and some of them had crumbled away. As
they approached the hovel, they became aware of a
stench rising from the earth, filling the air—the stench
of a corpse.

'What's that terrible smell?' exclaimed Hazil.

Rachmat glanced at him for a moment, turned away,
and looked at the three others. Isa couldn't stand it either.

'It's a dreadful smell—a dead chicken or dog perhaps,
that hasn't been buried.'

When Ontong heard Isa's words he laughed up-
roariously—brutally.

'That's no dog or hen,' he said. 'It's spies—two
Chinese women. We cut their throats three days ago.
They were caught passing through the village. They
were questioned and refused to talk. They said they
wanted to collect money owing them. What money?
Huh, this is what we did to them.' He moved his hand
towards his chopper, then with a forefinger drew a line
across his throat. He spat on the ground a thick clot of
mucus, like a marble. Kiran and Imam joined in the
laughter.

'Ontong is a real executioner. Neither of us would
have dared do it. He cut their throats,' said Kiran.

Throughout the conversation Rachmat remained
silent. He turned pale and kept his eyes averted from the
well.

'We threw them in the well. It stinks because you
didn't close it up properly,' said Ontong, scolding Iman

83

and Kiran. Isa felt an icy hand clutch at his heart. He was startled, filled with horror and terror. The air was thick with the breath of death. He looked at Hazil. Hazil's face was also tense and a little pale. His eyes were hard and cold.

In the few minutes since the conversation began Isa felt a terror he had never before experienced. Neither when he had hidden at Semedi's house during the clash with the Indian soldiers at Djalan Asam Lama, nor when he saw the wounded Chinese with his blood reddening like a tongue of fire in the darkness, nor even in the terror of his dreams had he felt anything as terrible as he felt now. All the terror that had befallen the two Chinese women was compressed in these sentences of Ontong who had not given the whole story of what had happened. It was the suggestion in Ontong's words, the tense face and body of Rachmat, the hard cold light in Hazil's eyes that did more violence to his thought and feelings than if the affair had been told him in detail.

His imagination went beyond the bounds of fact. His thoughts ran without hindrance and as fear rode upon them, the terror it created multiplied to infinity.

Isa's first instinct was to flee and in his struggle to control his fear and terror, he wet his pants. He did not dare to look into the well and quickly followed Hazil into the old hovel.

Rachmat's three companions were already lifting green boxes of ammunition from behind heaps of dried coconut fibre.

Isa and Hazil together carried a box of hand grenades, and three other boxes were carried by the three others. Rachmat followed behind them.

The villagers watched them, shouting in chorus 'Merdeka. Merdeka. Merdeka'. 'Dullah saw them coming, threw his cigarette to the ground and ran to greet them. He took the carrying cord of the grenade box from Isa. 'Let me take that,' he said.

After the boxes had been loaded onto the truck, Rachmat spoke again with the three others. They nodded, then went into the alley behind the lemonade factory and disappeared behind the shacks.

'You sit beside the driver,' said Hazil to Isa. 'The pair of us can get into the back'.

'No. We can all get in the back,' said Isa and they climbed up. Abdullah pressed the starter. This time the motor started at once, and Abdullah thought it worth his while to put out his head and shout to Hazil, proudly and gaily, 'It goes, doesn't it?'

They passed the KPM* Office near Gambir station, and Isa felt scared as he saw the Indian soldiers guarding the English headquarters looking at the truck as it passed.

At their feet were the boxes of ammunition and hand grenades, and the soldiers were standing at the side of the road. He did not feel relieved until Hazil waved his hand and cried 'Jai Hind'.† The Indian soldiers gave broad grins.

'The Sikhs', said Rachmat. The tenseness had left him and he took out cigarettes from his pocket and offered one to Hazil and Isa. Hazil took one but Isa refused. After striking a match a few times, Hazil lit it, and said suddenly:

'Those three must be dismissed from our organisation.'

---

*Initials of the Dutch inter-island packet service.
†Hail India. An Indian 'solidarity-making' slogan.

Rachmat suddenly went tense again.

'Had I dared I would have shot Ontong dead,' he said. 'I saw it all. From the beginning to the end.'

Isa saw that Rachmat was about to tell the story of the murder of the two Chinese women. His mouth opened to tell Rachmat to stop because he felt the terror descend on him again. But he restrained his instinct to blurt this out. It was as though he were obsessed by the desire to hear it in full.

'It happened three days ago. There were two Chinese women—a mother and her daughter—she was about sixteen. They passed the village. Everyone was put on the alert. Someone thought they were enemy spies. All the money they carried and their jewelry were stolen. I was helpless. The village people decided that they were spies without further investigation. They were dragged to the coconut plantation and Ontong cut their throats with his machete near the well—the night after they had been seized.

Isa felt his body become weak. 'Brutality. It's intolerable,' he said. His voice trembled, not with anger but with fear, fear. Not anger, but fear, fear fear, rose in his heart on hearing a story of such brutality.

'Anger is useless in a situation such as this,' said Hazil who had misunderstood what was behind Isa's words. 'Even protest is useless. It is beyond human control.'

'It can't be allowed, it's intolerable,' Isa's voice was trembling.

'There's no use in saying "it can't be". It has happened, and will happen again—again and again,' said Hazil. Rachmat did not say a word, his mouth tightly shut and his eyes fixed in front of him. 'Three days ago it happened to those innocent Chinese women. A week

86

ago it happened at Djati Petamburan. A little Eurasian girl of only eight was treated as a spy. Spies! Spies everywhere!! The day before yesterday at Kampung Bali there was an old Dutchman. As long as we have the Ontongs, Imans and Kirans this is going to happen. There are still too many of them among us, and it will be a long time before they vanish from our midst.'

The truck slowed down as it approached the Manggarai viaduct.

'To the right,' called Hazil to 'Dullah and he looked at Rachmat who was still silent. 'Don't let any of them know of our hideout at Manggarai. I don't trust people of that sort. They'd be as quick to betray us as they are ferocious now. Don't think too much about what happened. It's not your responsibility alone, it's that of all of us.'

'You don't think I was a coward to remain silent? asked Rachmat.

'What was there you could do? They would have cut your throat, too, if you had tried to stop them.'

Hazil ordered the truck to stop at a house by an intersection on a side road behind the Manggarai swimming-pool.

Four youths were waiting, sitting up on the verandah. They hurried out as they saw the truck stop.

'Merdeka'

'Quick, get everything inside,' said Hazil.

The road was empty. They hurriedly carried the boxes into the house. Not until they had finished was Isa introduced to the four young men—Amran, Djaja, Karim and Suroso. 'Do you understand everything?' Hazil asked Karim.

Karim nodded. 'They can go by train in four lots.

One of our people will go with them, and take them out at Krawang.' They shook hands again as they left. Rachmat stayed there.

The truck starter failed again so that the others had to come out of the house to help push. From other houses too people came out, seeing a push was needed. They all gave a hand.

'When all's said and done, you have to admit that our people are the best for "Gotong rojong"'* cried Abdullah as the machine burst into life and the truck sped homewards. 'It's easy to get help anywhere now— as long as we say it's for the Revolution.'

The other two didn't answer.

*Mutual help, collaboration.

6

'You'll get used to violence. Man has an extraordinary ability to adapt himself. Not only to killing in the line of duty, but even outside the line of duty—to blood and cruelty; everyone will grow used to it. It won't be long before Rachmat will think nothing of cutting off a human head—even though he will certainly never become a kind of person like Ontong,' said Hazil.

They were in the study in Isa's house. Hazil was standing near the window. The violin he had just been playing was in his hand. Isa was sitting behind the desk. He had brought up again the murder of the two Chinese women, saying that such cruelty had to be stamped out. Those responsible should be punished by the freedom fighters themselves. 'Murder should have no part in the struggle for freedom,' said Isa. 'I will never become used to violence,' he went on, 'I feel sick at the sight of it.'

'So you say now. But later you, too, will become used to it. How can you resist the force hurled upon us by the Dutch if you do not repay violence with violence?' asked Hazil.

Isa knew his answer—at least as far as it concerned himself. If he could, he would flee from violence or yield to it, so that violence itself would shelter him until he escaped. But he realised that he could not say this to Hazil. Hazil would be angry with him; and their friendship might be broken. Isa knew perfectly well that Hazil struggled with conviction and had staked all his flesh and blood.

No weapons had been transported since that occasion. Hazil said that the fourth box of grenades and ammunition had reached Krawang safely. After that afternoon at Asam Reges, for several nights Isa had been pursued by nightmares. He dreamt he had fallen into the deep, black, narrow well, and in the darkness he had fallen upon a pile of corpses and rotting bodies; even more terrifying, the faces of the bodies were his own. Now the dream returned only rarely. This did not mean that terror now was absent from his sleep. He still dreamt of a road with no end like a streak of lightning in utter darkness. And he ran half dead with panting, spurred onward by something terrifying that pursued him and which he did not understand. And to this dream was added that of the deep, black, narrow well.

'Let's try it again,' said Isa, avoiding Hazil's question.

Hazil placed the violin beneath his chin and played his composition again. The melody of the human pursuit of happiness he was still working on. And Isa beat the drum.

'What must be, must be.' 'We only die once.' 'When I first had to fire at someone, I wet myself.'

They laughed.

'Now you're too trigger happy.' 'If we don't shoot first, they'll shoot us.' 'And if you're dead, what's the point of it?' 'Death's the last thing you should think of.' 'Do you remember the Gurkha soldier picked off outside the brothel?'

They laughed again.

'He hadn't finished doing up his flies.'

They laughed again.

'The devil!' 'And the Japanese at Tangerang who cried "Banzai"* as the bamboo spear ripped open his stomach.' 'The Japanese certainly know how to die!' 'Yes, I never saw one of them ask for mercy or cry out when faced with death.' 'The best way to kill a person is with a bullet, it's clean and quick.' 'But there's no satisfaction in it. I prefer to cut the throat.' 'Oh, you're a one for blood.'

They laughed again.

It was night. In the alley where their truck had stopped, the street lights were all out. The doors and windows of all the houses were shut. Isa, sitting beside the driver, listened to the conversation of the youths with horror. Something terrifying was creeping into his heart. His body felt cold. He shuddered for a moment. He could not imagine himself ever able to take part in

*Long live Japan!

their banter about dying and death. The living should forget death, Never mention it, because it is neither beautiful nor attractive; but then neither is life. It is full of terror and menace and a pursuing fear—even in sleep and dreams. There is no release or respite from one day to the next—day or night; now and tomorrow and beyond tomorrow still further menace waits, behind it new fears.

The driver 'Dullah sitting beside him was tense. He, too, heard them making light of dying and death. He, too, was afraid. As he drew on his cigarette from time to time, the tip glowed lighting up the outline of his coarse face. Isa tried to fathom the feelings reflected there. But it was expressionless. And Isa felt the more isolated and alone in the clutches of his fear.

Again the conversation of the three youths standing at the edge of the road near the truck came to Isa's ears.

'I should be dead already,' said one of them, 'several times. Do you remember the NICA attack on the Police Post at Karet? I was there. All the police were shot and beheaded. I wasn't even touched. I lay motionless near the body of a policeman. They paid no particular attention and went off. Then during the clash at Tanah Tinggi a man beside me was hit. I wasn't touched. Now I don't think of death any more. I've been lucky.'

'Don't be too sure,' said another. 'Death cannot be held off. Not by you. By none of us.'

The first speaker laughed. 'Even if we are all killed, we cannot be stopped.'

And Isa thought of the road with no end. Once foot

had been set on it, the journey had to be continued without end. The road of his fear. He was afraid to join them talking about death, and was even more afraid not to join them.

Even though he had now long been with these youths of the Revolution who could talk lightly of death, Isa still could find no joy in his heart for the Struggle. His fear would not allow him any feeling of enthusiasm.

Hazil came out from the alley close to where the truck had stopped.

'They haven't brought the weapons here yet. The Indians who were going to sell them didn't turn up yesterday. Let's go back.'

The trio who were laughing at death and dying leapt into the back of the truck and Hazil sat beside Isa closely wedged together with the driver. Abdullah pressed the starter, but the engine didn't fire. He pressed it again. There was only the sound of the starter engine. Hazil leapt down and Isa followed him.

'Suroso, Djaja, Amran, push.' Hazil called to the three of them who had already started to get out.

'Devil of a truck,' growled Amran, frustrated.

The other two laughed.

As they were pushing the truck Isa shuddered again for a moment. He remembered his first meeting with these three youths who made light of death; when Hazil, Rachmat and himself were carrying four boxes of grenades and ammunition to Manggarai.

At that meeting he never imagined the youths could talk like that, from without they appeared like other young people. There was no sign of cruelty in their faces. Isa felt he was in an unknown world—pushing the truck together with strangers. The only one he knew was Hazil; but all he knew of Hazil was his music. Everything apart from the music was a mystery to him.

That night he pushed the truck, panting because it was a long time before the engine sprang to life. Pushing the truck with companions who were strangers to him.

JANUARY 1947·

Isa turned over and over the dirty envelope in his hands. It contained a letter from Hazil—from Krawang, brought by Rachmat—Rachmat said he was coming to his house that afternoon. Outside was the uproar of the school-children playing during the recess. The classroom was empty.

As Isa was about to open the letter Saleh came in.

'Isa,' he said, 'I want to ask your advice.' He sat on a bench in front of Isa's desk.

'Yes?' said Isa raising his head and looking at him.

'I want to get out.'

'Get out?' asked Isa. His interest was aroused. The words sounded sweet to him. To evacuate—to flee from all of this. Flee from Djakarta, full of menace and shooting—from death, rapine and violence.

'I want to move to Purwakarta. To my parent's place. I can't stand this any longer—no sleep at night. Police raids every moment. Yesterday the NICA arrested one of my neighbours.'

'Does the Head agree?'

'Yes. He said he can't hold me if I want to go. It only means I have to resign because he can't give me leave.'

'Have you resigned?'

'Yes. I'm going to look for another job at Purwakarta. Who can carry on like this?'

Isa felt relieved. Now he realised he was not alone in his fear. Saleh, too, was afraid. So were others. They were all afraid. Why don't I evacuate too? I'll be free. I'll be my old self again, thought Isa. He smiled.

'In that case, I think you'd better go,' he said.

'And how about you?' Saleh asked him.

'I must think first.' Isa replied. He felt an extraordinary pleasure in the role he was playing.

Saleh was relieved that Isa agreed with his plan to leave his job and find refuge outside the city.

He praised Isa. 'It's astonishing how you can remain calm in this terrifying atmosphere.'

Isa was startled. He suspected Saleh was making fun of him. He looked at Saleh's face; but there was no light of mirth in his eyes.

Isa's feeling of pleasure returned.

'One can only do one's duty in such a situation,' he said simply. It was rarely that he spoke thus.

Saleh shook his hand and left as the bell went summoning the children back to the classroom.

As he taught, his mind often wandered, thinking how pleasant it would be if he too could evacuate. At the same time, Hazil's letter lying on the table also distracted him. What had Hazil to say?

After school Isa sat behind his desk pretending to be busy marking the pupils' work. He waited until all the other teachers had gone home. The school was deserted. Isa continued marking the Arithmetic. When he was sure everyone had gone he quickly got up and went to the cupboard.

He took from it ten new exercise books and placed them deftly in his briefcase. Every time he had done this, a feeling of shame at stealing disturbed him. But it had grown steadily less. Today he hardly felt it at all.

For a moment he recalled Hazil's words that man could become used to anything—to violence, to murder, even to theft.

He realised that he still hadn't read Hazil's letter. He quickly opened it.

'Isa,' Hazil wrote, 'I have been almost a month at Krawang now, and this is the first time I have had the chance to give you news. We have been very busy organising and training the People's Army through the whole Krawang area. There is so much to do and so few people to do it, people who are good, able and trustworthy. My first idea in writing was to tell you about the excitement and the vitality of the Revolution, just that. So that you could share it with us. But that would not be the whole story and I would deceive both you and myself if I told you only what was good. Of course, many of our people have high ideals, but I am coming to see more and more people using the Revolution as a guise to feather their own nests. How many petty War Lords have sprung up! Leaders of all sorts of armed groups with no respect for anything. Many of them oppress the people with demands for rice, meat and money. And the cruelty they perpetrate! Sometimes I am filled with shame to think that we revile and condemn the terror done by the NICA in Djakarta, yet are guilty of the same wickedness against our own people.

'I must tell you of a pointless, cruel and unnecessary slaying, committed just as you might flick off and kill an ant. Just like that. He was a village pedlar. I don't know his name. He came from Djakarta carrying bundles of cloth, shirts and vests—the usual village pedlar. They seized him at Bekasi and took him from the train. He was taken to the Headquarters of a company of irregulars. They went through all his wares and found a towel with an edging of red, white and blue round the brand name. That night he was executed—just like that. I got the story from Rachmat who seems fated to witness such acts of cruelty against his fellow men. He didn't see the actual execution but he was present at the investigation and the sentence. Now we are frightened even of ourselves. Everyone is suspected of being an enemy spy.

'Rachmat now can keep company with violence. He is one of our bravest men. And even though he doesn't say much his feelings are deep. Only, every day he grows more taciturn. Karim, you surely remember him, was shot and seriously wounded in a clash with an enemy patrol near Bekasi. Now he is in the military hospital at Purwakarta. Send him a few newspapers via Rachmat, if they are available.

'This Revolution is like a flood and now no-one can control its course. Whatever we do, it follows it own road, heedless of us who created it. I have been out of Djakarta for a month because I heard that the NEFIS* and the English Field Security are looking for me. There is terror here too—only in a different form. Now I'm not afraid of being hunted down by the NEFIS or the Field Security. There are other fears in various guises. I fear we are not strong enough and of sufficient stature to persevere on this road with no end we have chosen. Can a man who is full of fear achieve anything worthwhile in a world full of fear?

'All kinds of fears menace us from all directions, but now I can laugh at myself again. Why should I run

*The Dutch Intelligence Service.

from Djakarta because I am afraid of the NEFIS and the Field Security? We cannot flee from everything. So when my work here is finished I'm coming back to Djakarta. I'm longing to play my music again—even though I've never really been separated from it while I've been here. Indeed, I have had many new experiences in the midst of our people which have helped me to develop it. But burn this letter after you have read it. And this is another fear—that it may fall into the hands of someone who can do us harm. But this I hope is a healthy fear.

'Actually, there is still much that I want to tell you about conditions here. It's all fascinating even though much is terrifying. Rachmat will tell you about other matters.

'My greetings,' wrote Hazil, 'and my regards to Fatima.' And so he ended his letter.

Isa tapped the letter against the table—he felt restless. He thought of Saleh who was going to evacuate. Even so, thought Isa, there would be no safety. Suddenly he felt depressed. It was as though it was he who had decided to evacuate and now realised that evacuation would not help him. His fear of remaining in Djakarta, with a salary every day more inadequate, and of the terror of NICA every moment of the day and night suddenly bore down on him with overwhelming force. He was oppressed by fear, like a man hurled into the condemned cell and the door slammed shut. He could no longer flee—ever. Indeed, deep in his heart he had long been thinking of flight, of flight from all his fears. Earlier that morning Saleh had given him hope; but Hazil's letter had destroyed it.

He crumpled up the letter in his hand, then got up

to call the school janitor. He asked him for a match and burnt the letter in front of him.

He ground the black ash into the ground with his heel.

After selling the exercise books at the Chinese store in Pasar Tanah Abang, Isa hurried home.

'So, even though the Linggadjati agreement has been initialled, those in the interior do not believe that it will achieve anything. The principal question is that of fixed, regular and guaranteed communication between those in the city and those outside,' said Rachmat.

They were in Isa's study.

'Our work all this time has been inadequate because of poor organisation. Now we have collected sufficient funds to administer our work we must co-ordinate our efforts both in the city and the country. We must separate those purchasing, those who deliver to those who store, and those who store to deliver to those outside. In this way we hope to lessen the risk involved because when the same people are responsible for every stage of the operation, danger of discovery is much greater. It has been decided that you are to be responsible for funds for Djakarta, and from time to time someone will come to ask you for money with letters and official documentation from our Headquarters at Krawang.'

Isa was taken aback. His first reaction had been to refuse. He knew that if he accepted he would be plunged into an atmosphere of even greater menace and danger. Could he refuse? How could he refuse?—he asked himself. He was afraid to refuse—afraid he would be accused of treachery. If he accepted, disaster would fall upon him, if he refused, an even greater disaster.

He didn't see any sign of query or doubt in the hard lines of Rachmat's face. Rachmat acted as if it were a matter of course that Isa would accept without any question or hesitation. To Rachmat this was a duty. It did not occur to him for a moment that it could or might be rejected. Aware that if Isa accepted body and soul might be broken, yet sure nonetheless that Isa would accept; because it was inevitable.

Isa could only say 'All right. When will the money be sent? Have you got it with you?'

'No. Hazil will bring it later.'

'When will he come?' he asked hopefully.

'I don't know. He said in the next week or so. Be very careful now because the NEFIS is expanding its field of operations and sharpening its skills,' said Rachmat, bringing their conversation to a close, and once again arousing terror in Isa's heart.

That night Isa slept restlessly. He dreamt that terrifying shapes of men cloaked in black were trying to enter his house. He awoke, leapt out of bed, and tried to lock all the windows and doors. But all his keys broke and in a cold sweat of terror he tried to tie up the windows with string. From without, the men cloaked in black began to pound on the windows and doors. The strings he had just tied broke, one by one. A window began to open, slowly, and a hand groped into the room . . . With a start Isa awoke . . . He was awake. His heart thudded so violently that his chest ached and all his nerves trembled as he waited in the darkness, the terror of the dream still shrouding his mind. Time flowed over him until eventually he realised he had been dreaming. A feeling of relief soothed his feelings and his heart drank up the relief, like parched ground tormented by the heat of the sun soaking up a heavy shower of rain.

It was a long time before he fell asleep again.

During the night the sound of gunfire broke the silence.

FEBRUARY

Very early, at five o'clock in the morning, the soldiers were ready. Five of their big trucks left the barracks of Battalion X at dawn when everything was still wet with dew. One truck was completely closed in with heavy green canvas, They turned to the intersection of Kebon Sirih with Pasar Senen, turned into Tjideng and stopped in front of the Nimef canning factory. The soldiers leapt out and began an encircling movement of the village around the factory. The covered truck stopped at the cross-roads in front of the factory building.

A few vegetable vendors coming from the station were taken by surprise; they were arrested, and ordered to assemble near the truck parked at the cross-roads. All their loads were unfastened and checked. Then they were allowed to proceed.

Other soldiers entered the alleys of the village knocking at doors. All the men were ordered out and taken across to the covered truck.

The road became crowded. A few frightened women began to cry. So did their children. And the dogs barked. A few men who tried to run were caught, beaten by the soldiers, and ordered to file past the covered truck. Despite the early hour the street was crowded. The men had been startled from their sleep. Many were wearing only their underpants and vests; their hair was tousled and their faces unwashed.

All had to file past the truck as they turned back towards their houses. One man was picked out and ordered to stand at the side of the road. Another two were taken, and ordered to stand beside him. The remainder continued to file past the truck.

'A search,' said the first man to the second.

'Who is the traitor?' said the second. His face was pale but his voice did not tremble.

'Yesterday they did the same at Tanah Tinggi,' said the third. He was the most calm.

'In that truck is a traitor who knows the young people in the village who have joined the Struggle,' he continued.

'Who is it in the truck this time?' He shrugged his shoulders and spat on the ground.

Five more were taken from the stream of men filing past the truck and made to join them. The eight looked at each other. They all knew each other. And they knew who among them had taken part and who had not.

'If you are freed later,' said one who knew what he could expect from his captors, to one of those who had not taken part, 'remember me to my Mother. Tell her not to worry. The worst that can happen is imprisonment in Bukitduri. There's nothing to it.' He managed an unconvincing laugh.

A soldier approached them and shouted 'You must not speak. Shut up!'

They were silent. Then they were ordered into a truck. The search was over. The truck carrying the soldiers and the eight prisoners sped off. The main road remained deserted and in eight houses a few women wept with fear and terror. That was all.

MARCH

'There's no more rice. Don't forget to ask for an advance,' Fatima called to Isa as he went down the steps on his way to school.

Her husband nodded. During these last few months, even rice had joined the horrible nightmares disturbing his sleep every night. Several times he dreamt of mountains of rice falling upon and crushing him. He had become rather thin. Behind his eyes was buried a terror which he tried to conceal and lock deep within himself. His other dreams—a lightning glimpse of the road with no end in a black night, the dead Chinese, the well filled with bodies, continued to pursue him.

Often now, if he heard any news that disturbed him, his heart beat and thudded till his chest ached.

At night he was afraid to go to bed because of the terror lurking behind the curtain of his dreams. He longed to tell Fatima everything, but fear restrained him. Fatima would laugh at him—or refuse to listen; and that would be even worse.

When Fatima said once again that there was no more rice, his heart thudded. He put his hands on his chest to control the aching, and without looking round, replied, 'All right.'

In front of Hamidy's house Isa stopped. He didn't want to get to school yet. He wanted time for the thudding of his heart to subside. He opened the gate on the bamboo fence which squeaked as though it were hung on a rusty hinge.

Hamidy opened the door after a few knocks. 'Merdeka,' said Isa.

'Merdeka, how are things?'

'May we borrow your truck this afternoon?' asked Isa.

Hamidy was silent. He looked away from Isa's face,

pretending to be thinking. He stroked his chin and eventually said:

'Not this afternoon, I've promised it to someone else. Any other day, of course.'

'But this is very important for our Struggle,' said Isa.

Hamidy looked at him—'Hasn't the Linggadjati agreement been signed? How can we carry on fighting? Haven't we been ordered to lay down arms?'

Isa didn't answer because these were his own feelings. Feelings which he echoed fully and profoundly. When the Linggadjati agreement was signed with full ceremonial on the 25th of March, Isa had sipped for a moment the cool air of Freedom.

'Now we can relax again,' he said to Fatima when the news of the signing was announced. He had made all kinds of plans: to buy a new dress for Fatima, new shoes for Salim, a new mattress for their bed to replace the old patched one. The nights following the Linggadjati agreement were free from terrifying nightmares, but his freedom did not last long.

'Now we must redouble our efforts,' Hazil said to him, a few days after the Agreement had been signed. He had arrived back in Djakarta from Krawang a few days after the signature.

'Don't forget that the Dutch launched an attack on Modjokerto before the Agreement was signed,' said Hazil when Isa protested saying that now peace had come.

After that conversation, his terrifying nightmares returned, undiminished in intensity. His only relaxation was to play music with Hazil. These were the moments when he could forget rice—forget his dreams —forget the road with no end—forget the shot Chinese

—forget the well filled with bodies and forget Fatima.

Isa took his leave of Hamidy. The gate of the bamboo fence squeaked again as he went out. The Chinese salesman standing in front of his stall greeted him and Isa returned the greeting.

Only when he was sitting in the tram did Isa think of something. Rather, there was something slipped his mind which he could not remember. The previous morning, Pak Damrah had not been selling his wares at the corner by the crossroads. On the main road they passed three truck loads of soldiers, who shook their fists at the passengers on the tram and hurled insults.

Isa recalled again Hazil's words—'Now all the British troops have gone. The Dutch used the Linggadjati Agreement only to cheat the world at large. We must lose no time in making our preparations.' Hazil had thumped the table with his fist and said 'We still don't have the funds. They only talk, plan this and that. But nothing comes of it. The decisions were made in January, now it's almost the end of March and we still don't have a cent. Bah!'

Isa repressed his feelings of relief at hearing this. He was glad there were no funds for him to take charge of.

When Rachmat had come with the plan for funds for the Struggle, Isa had been in fear of the moment when he would have to take responsibility for large sums of money. But a month had gone by and still no-one had brought the money; thus he felt relieved. And now he felt even more relieved.

That day, he had taught with more zest. After school he waited until all the teachers had gone, and when the school was empty, he opened the cupboard, took twenty new exercise books and put them into his briefcase.

Isa had just come back from school. As he was taking off his coat in the bedroom, Fatima came from the kitchen and said:

'Isa, do you know that Hamidy next door has evacuated? To Jogja, leaving his uncle to look after the house.'

'Evacuated? When?' Isa's heart thudded. He was startled and afraid. 'Why?' His voice was muffled because he was drawing his shirt over his head.

'He left this morning by train.'

'Did he come here?'

'No. His uncle told me, after he had gone.'

Isa was silent. He took a pair of pyjamas from the cupboard; they were threadbare, and the stripes were faded. He took off his street trousers, sat on the edge of the bed and took off his shoes. He had had to do without socks for a long time.

'Why did he have to evacuate? I don't understand,' said Isa.

'Perhaps he was afraid,' replied Fatima.

'What did he have to be afraid of? Isn't there a treaty between the Republic and the Dutch now?'

'His uncle said he was afraid because the Dutch are still carrying out arrests. He said that Hamidy had received a lot of goods from the Japanese—he has a whole warehouse full in the city. Now the Dutch are searching for them.'

'What sort of things?'

'I don't know. The uncle said that the warehouse used to belong to a Dutch importer.'

'How can the Dutch know?'

'The Japanese gave the contents of the warehouse to

Hamidy. Perhaps the Japanese told them.'

'May be'.

Then he remembered something and felt even more afraid.

'Perhaps Damrah too has evacuated. It's several mornings now since I saw him on my way to school.'

'Lots of people have evacuated,' said Fatima. 'The medical assistant in Alley No. 5 has gone. They've all gone. They've just left their houses and asked their neighbours to look after them.'

Isa was silent. He put on his pyjama trousers.

'How about if we evacuate?' he said suddenly. He spoke without conviction because he himself was as much afraid to go into the interior as to stay on in Djakarta; if there was a choice it was better to live with the terror which he knew. The terror he did not know was far more terrifying. Stories of the ferocity of the irregulars froze his inclination to evacuate. He himself didn't know why he said what he did, suggesting that he and Fatima evacuate. He himself had no real desire to do so. The interior was fraught with menace as great as that in the city. What was the use of running from a fear he knew to a strange one? But his question was more or less an inevitable continuation of words which had to be uttered in the course of their conversation once it had begun in the way it did. So he felt relieved when Fatima said 'What's the use of joining the evacuees? If we're going to die, we may as well die here.'

Hearing the word death, Isa felt afraid again. In his mind's eye he saw himself sprawling in the dry dust, blood flowing from a wound in his chest. He was silent.

'Yes, why should we follow others?' he said, even

though in his heart he was screaming to run, run and run into the ultimate distance.

Isa always had a poor appetite, but that day he ate so little that Fatima asked him, 'What's wrong? Are you ill?'

'I don't feel well. I have been feverish since yesterday.'

'Malaria again, perhaps?' said Fatima. 'Take a quinine tablet. There are still some in the cupboard.'

Isa pushed his plate to the middle of the table and gulped down his glass of tea. 'I think I'll lie down,' he said. 'If Hazil comes, tell him I'm ill.'

But Hazil didn't come. In the evening, Isa's fever grew worse and he went hot and cold. It's malaria, he said to himself in his fever. Two days went by; he was confined to bed, and Hazil still didn't come. He lay ill for five days and five nights, and as his fever rose all kinds of thoughts and fantasies came to disturb him, visions and dreams of fear and terror. When the fever left him and he felt wrung out, his mind was a little more at rest, as he lay there relaxed. He knew that as long as he was ill, Fatima would not disturb him with money matters, or 'no rice' or other things of that kind. He also knew that Hazil would not be able to ask him to do anything dangerous and frightening. And it was not until the fifth day, when his fever had broken that Hazil arrived. The fever had gone; he felt light and weak. It was as though the strength had been drained from all his muscles, but he felt a certain satisfaction in this helplessness. There was a buzzing sound in his ears because of the quinine tablets. His head was light and a little dizzy, but he was glad to have been ill.

But now the fever had almost run its course, he could

not lie content in bed. He began to hate the sight of the filthy patched mosquito net and the grubby patched sheet. He forced himself to get up and went to sit in the dining-room. Fatima made the bed.

It was then that Hazil entered. 'Merdeka', he called opening the door, and seeing Isa pale and listless, leaning back in a chair, he hurriedly approached him and took his hand.

'Have you been ill? I didn't know.'

'Malaria,' said Isa smiling faintly. 'But I am almost better now—only still weak. My head is aching.'

He rubbed his forehead with his hand.

'Sit down,' he said to Hazil. Fatima stood at the door of the bedroom.

'So now you've come?' she said. 'Where have you been all this time?' She didn't wait for an answer, but quickly went back into the room to carry on with her work.

Isa looked at Hazil. Now he has a new job for me, he thought fearfully. Hazil looked at him with his sunken eyes and pale lips, his whole body a picture of weakness, and thought: This comrade is a very sick man, far more sick than he realises. And as this passed through his mind, without knowing why, his thoughts turned to Fatima. Her body was fresh and youthful and full of the fire of life. And Isa was sick, very sick. Hazil repressed these thoughts as deeply as he could.

'There's still no news of our funds,' said Hazil dejectedly.

Isa felt relieved again.

'What's going on then?' he asked.

'Things are going from bad to worse,' said Hazil. 'Rachmat was almost caught when the NICA soldiers carried out a search of Gang Sentiong. It was only a matter of five minutes. He had just left when a truck filled with soldiers arrived and stopped in front of the house where he lodged. It was one of the first to be searched. An old man in the house was arrested, together with several youths. He's back home now, but he told everything—all Rachmat's activities. I met him after his release, weeping, begging forgiveness, and saying he had been tortured. Fortunately he only knew about Rachmat.'

'Tortured?' asked Isa with all his fears flooding back to him, flowing together, setting his heart thudding.

'Yes. Kicked and beaten. His lips were split. After he had told all Rachmat's activities and about smuggling weapons to Bekasi, he was beaten again because they wanted to know the names of others besides Rachmat. Only after he fainted several times because there was nothing more he knew, did they stop torturing him.'

'Where is Rachmat now?'

'He's at my house waiting for a chance to get out of the city.'

'Your father?'

'He has nothing to say now. The old people have given way to the young—so he said when I got back from Krawang. Apparently, while I was away, he thought things through and decided to give way to the young generation. "We who are old must give way to you who are young," that's what he said to me' Hazil laughed.

The story of the old man from Gang Sentiong, captured and tortured by the Dutch, made Isa's heart tremble. In the imagination of his terror, at any moment the NICA soldiers were about to swoop on Kebon Sireh, arrest him and take him away. This very moment—now—they would arrive. His stomach felt hollow with fear. Then he thought, I am still ill. How can they arrest someone ill?

But this only gave him a moment's comfort. His fear increased, and his body, just striken, was not strong enough to control the chill of fear which set his whole body quivering.

Hazil looked at him. 'You are ill again', he said. I've made you tired. Lie down again.'

'My head is aching,' said Isa, trying to keep the tremor from his voice.

Hazil stood up, helped Isa to his feet and led him to the bedroom. As he opened the bedroom door, standing behind Isa he caught a glimpse of Fatima in the mirror, her breast half exposed. She quickly covered her breast with her kebaja and, turning quickly, walked over to meet them. But for a moment her eyes had met Hazil's meaningfully in the mirror.

'What is it, Isa?' she asked her husband, as she fixed a pillow for Isa on the bed. This was the first time Hazil had been into their bedroom. Suddenly, he felt different—as though between him and Fatima a new and more intimate relationship had developed, between them alone. Up to then, Isa as her husband had always been present at their meetings. But on this occasion, Isa had no place in Hazil's thoughts. There was only Fatima and himself. He now saw articles of women's clothing that a man rarely sees, unless he is a husband or perhaps a lover. A brassiere hanging from the towel-rail, a waist sash half-rolled on the dressing-table, a box of powder, a comb with several teeth broken.

Isa lay down on the bed. 'Rest,' said Hazil, 'I won't stay long. You're just better, and need a lot of rest.'

Hazil walked out of the room; Fatima followed him and turned towards the kitchen. Hazil was doubtful for a moment and on the point of leaving; but at the sight of Fatima going to the kitchen, he followed her.

She was trying to light the fire under the stove. 'Inah bought wet wood again,' she sighed, looking up, feeling Hazil's presence in the doorway, and then blew into the smoke-filled stove. Her eyes stung and watered. She avoided Hazil's gaze to prevent a repetition of the meeting of their eyes in the mirror.

'Let me help,' said Hazil, bending himself down and crouching beside her. Fatima shifted her position and moved away a little. Hazil pretended not to see. He blew the fire strongly. After a few puffs and after his eyes too had watered with the acridity of the smoke, the fire caught. He clapped his hands, covered with ash and turning to Fatima, said 'Look—it's alight now.' Fatima smiled at him.

'Thanks, you're clever.'

She placed the pot filled with water on the stove and said 'Inah's been a long time at the stall. I'm sure she's gossiping again. She always does.'

Hazil did not answer and for a moment the kitchen was silent apart from the crackling of the fire. Suddenly they realised they were alone in the small, hot kitchen—quite alone. Hazil looked at Fatima and she looked at him. Both suddenly felt the atmosphere had become tense and meaningful.

They smiled at each other—the atmosphere eased. The tension had been absorbed into their bodies and left them filled with happiness. Their hearts were light and they thought only of each other. 'Let me help,' said Hazil, seizing Fatima's hand and taking the wood from

112

her grasp. He peeled off the bark still adhering to it and said, 'If the wood is wet, take off the bark because it is the bark which absorbs water. I learnt that when I was a scout.'

'You've got soot on your fingers,' he said, after putting the wood into the stove, and his hand took Fatima's again. As he drew her hand towards him, he felt a resistance in her, but he continued to draw it closer as though urging her to him and felt the resistance gradually slacken. Her full, firm breast pressed against his side. He bent his head, his lips seeking her mouth; but she turned her face away and Hazil was able only to brush her cheek with his lips.

Suddenly she jerked herself out of his embrace, stood up, stepped back a pace and whispered, trembling, 'Don't.' Her breasts rose and fell, her cheeks flushed and her eyes became moist. Hazil acted as if nothing had happened. He took another piece of wood, peeled off the bark and carefully placed it in the stove. Then he blew the fire so that it burnt more brightly. 'Your fire won't go out again now,' he said, standing up, dusting the seat of his pants. 'And now I must go.' He looked at Fatima. For a moment their eyes met. Then Hazil smiled, and gradually a smile formed on Fatima's lips. They both understood.

Those days in May, when the servant girl Inah was out, were blissfully happy for Hazil and Fatima. While Isa was ill, Hazil came often with fruit and delicacies for him. Now Isa was better—even though he was still somewhat weak. But he insisted on going back to teach; and because it had become a habit, Hazil still came to the house while he was at school.

The first time, Hazil felt a little strange and Fatima realised it.

'I must go to the kitchen first,' she said.

'I'll have some music,' said Hazil, and he went to Isa's study. He had hardly started playing the violin when he heard Fatima calling him from the bedroom.

'Hazil, help me again. The fire won't light and Inah is out.'

Hazil stepped to the bedroom door.

'May I pass through here?' he asked.

'Why not?' said Fatima. He placed the violin on Isa's desk and went into the bedroom. Fatima was standing next to the bed. Their eyes met. Hazil walked slowly and stood before her, looking for a long time into her face, until she lowered her eyes; Hazil took her in his arms and whispered 'Fatima'. At first she tried to release herself, but without much effort or conviction, whispering: 'We are sinning, sinning.' Her words vanished, swallowed in Hazil's kisses and at length she yielded—yielded—yielded.

A while later they were in the kitchen lighting the fire. Fatima felt happy. She had no regrets, rather she felt relieved that none of the anxiety, regret or fear she had expected came to disturb her. 'Don't forget your pipe,' she said, and fetched it from the bed where he had left it.

Hazil thought of this as he took it from his pocket and lit it with a stump of burning wood. He acted quite naturally, too, and this helped Fatima.

When Isa came home from school, nothing happened. They were quite natural together, and Isa did not notice anything. He only said, 'Have you been here long?'

'Since this morning. I've been playing the violin.'

'Shall we play after our meal?' asked Isa and Hazil nodded. And after eating they made music.

That was how it began. How long can this go on? Hazil asked himself as he lay on Isa's bed and Fatima standing beside him, was fixing her kain.*

'Get up quickly, lazy bones', said Fatima. 'Salim will be home in a moment.'

Their relationship, he thought, was rather strange. Neither of them mentioned the word 'love'. And they were able to talk of Isa without emotion—as though he were not Fatima's husband but a third person, a mutual friend, who was to be pitied and, therefore, stood in need of affection and shelter.

Once Fatima said to him, 'Hazil, Isa is always afraid. He does not know that I often hear him scream in his sleep and cry out in terror.'

'Who isn't afraid?' he answered. 'I, too, am afraid. Where is there anyone not afraid? But this Revolution must go on. Individually we can be defeated, crushed by the enemy; but together, you and I, with Isa, Rachmat and the others, we are strong. This huge burden of fear we can divide among us into something we can carry between us and prevent it from paralysing our hearts and minds. Our fear weighs heavily upon us now because many of our people are reluctant to join us, and some are even helping the enemy. But even though alone, still we must go on. We may die—our comrades in arms may die, but we must go on. If we halt, we are defeated even if still alive. Because in revolution, even

*Sarong-like garment extending from waist to ankles.

death is a kind of victory. The enemy cannot rule our minds for ever.

'But if one is always scared, like Isa?' asked Fatima again.

'Man must learn to conquer his fear. Fear after all is a healthy emotion and our duty is to overcome it—Isa has to. It would be worse for him now if we withdrew him from the Struggle because he would never again get an opportunity to grapple with his fear; he would remain a coward all his life. We don't want that to happen do we?'

This concluded their discussion of Isa. That was in June, but now it was July and as he lay on the bed, watching Fatima replacing first her kain, then the brassiere enclosing her firm, round white breasts, he knew that days such as this were almost over. Rumours that the Dutch were planning an attack the following month multiplied. Only the date was not certain. Some said it would be the fifteenth—others the twenty-fifth.

The fifteenth had come and gone. Everyone was waiting for the twenty-fifth. This was the nineteenth. Hazil decided not to say anything to Fatima. Suddenly he jumped up from the bed as he heard Salim calling from outside. He left the bedroom and sat at Isa's desk. Fatima gave a little laugh. She took Hazil's pipe from under the pillow and handed it to him. 'You always forget,' she said.

7

'This may be the last time Fatima,' said Hazil, getting up from the bed. 'I didn't tell you before because I didn't want to worry you. But after the Dutch launched their attack on the twenty-first we had to begin operations inside the city. I can't come so often now.'

He strode out of the room onto the verandah. Fatima followed him. At the door, Hazil stopped and took her hand.

'Tell Isa he has to be ready.'

Fatima looked anxiously at him.

'Be careful,' she said. Hazil laughed.

'As though I were walking upon eggs,' he said. 'I want to kiss you again—your lips, all of you.'

He leapt down and hurried to the alley and vanished out of her sight. For a long time Fatima stood at the door watching the empty alley.

When Isa came back from school, Fatima wasn't at

home. He called her several times, but only the servant girl Inah appeared. 'Madame has gone to the Hakim's in Laan Holle. Will you eat first?' Isa nodded. 'Set the table,' he said.

He went into the bedroom, put his briefcase on the desk, and stood by the window. He took off his shirt and stood in his vest with a tear in the back. Then he sat on the bed, bent down and took off his shoes. Barefooted, he went to the bathroom to wash his hands and face. He returned to the bedroom and took a sarong from the towel-rail.

Isa soon finished eating. Since his illness he had had little appetite; and after the Dutch had launched their attack against the Indonesian Republic a few days earlier, his nerves had become even worse. He was easily startled, and then he felt an aching pain under his heart, draining the life from his body. He felt weak and shaky.

He lay on the bed. The room was stuffy. He got up again and went to get a book from the bookcase in his study. From the wardrobe he took a handkerchief. Then he lay down again. He didn't have the energy to read for long. His head was aching. He wiped his face with a handkerchief and placed it under the pillow. As he did so, his fingers closed on something hard. Isa took the hard object out and saw he was holding a pipe.

He was baffled. What was a pipe doing under the pillow? It was some time before he realised as he gazed on the pipe that it belonged to Hazil. But he did not at once realise the significance of its presence under the pillow. As the truth became clear to him, his first reaction was fury, and a desire to destroy them both. He leapt up and went out of the room to call Fatima. But

118

she was out. He walked up and down from one room to the other, a raging fire in his heart coursing through his body. His head was splitting. The anguished thudding of his heart returned, and he was forced to sit on the side of the bed, the pipe still in his hand.

'They've been having an affair,' he said.

'But perhaps not—perhaps Hazil just needed to rest and forgot his pipe.

'He has never slept here all this time,' he said.

'They're having an affair,' he said.

'But perhaps he just lay down alone and forgot his pipe.'

'They've slept together,' he said.

'They haven't.'

'They have. They haven't. Yes—No—Yes—No—No.'

At length Isa realised he could never know the meaning of the pipe under the pillow. It merely became one thing more in his life, to become part of his imagination to add to his nightly terror when he was alone with his thoughts and dreams. A cold sweat drenched his body, and now Isa felt that he was the guilty one and hurriedly, with a trembling heart, put the pipe into a drawer of his desk, locked it and put the key into his wallet. He would not ask. He was afraid to ask—afraid that if he asked he would find out that what he suspected had really happened; and that, and everything which would stem from it, was more terrifying to him than his present uncertainty. So he put away the pipe and kept his mouth shut. Yet he also knew that he could not shut and lock his mind. And from that moment, he trembled as he thought of the terror of the pipe which would always pursue him along the road with no end.

Isa lay down again on the bed.

When Fatima returned, towards evening, she saw that Isa was sleeping feverishly.

'Isa, has your malaria returned?' she asked him. And as she forced two quinine pills into his mouth Isa remained silent.

That night, as she slept beside him, Isa felt she was a stranger to him—and he felt unutterably alone.

It was not until three days later that Hazil came again, early in the morning. Hearing from Fatima that Isa was ill, he hurried into the room. 'Malaria again,' Isa said to him. 'Hell,' said Hazil. 'We need everyone we can muster now.'

In his heart Isa felt relieved he was ill. Well, you can't use me, he thought contentedly. 'I'm willing enough now,' he said to Hazil,' but I'm still weak and the fever keeps recurring.'

'Get well soon,' said Hazil. 'We're all counting on you.' Isa felt even happier.

'If you can't make it I'll have to find someone else,' said Hazil. He patted Isa's hand and walked out of the room. Then he asked Fatima, lowering his voice, 'Did you see my pipe under the pillow?'

Fatima went pale.

'Did you forget it again?'

'I don't know whether I left it here or at a friend's house . . . or lost it on the road.' Fatima was relieved.

'Perhaps you lost it on the road or left it somewhere else. I haven't seen it.'

'I was only afraid *he* might have found it' said Hazil.

'It's not here' said Fatima.

'All right. I must go now,' said Hazil.

In the bedroom, Isa could hear their conversation.

Their voices reached him faintly and he struggled to catch what they were talking about. For a moment the fire blazed up again in his heart—the fire which blazed in his heart when he first found the pipe under the pillow, but it quickly sank down again. He clenched his fists tight and struck his head savagely.

8

It was night at Pasar Senen. Saturday night. The Kramat square was very crowded. There was only one house at the cinema because the curfew had been extended.

'Another quarter of an hour' said Hazil, drinking down his beer. Rachmat and Isa were sitting at a table with him, looking at each other.

There had long been a chill in Isa's stomach. He wished he were a thousand miles away, away from the restaurant, from the Rex Cinema. His stomach was distended with wind and his heart was beating so fast that the thudding hurt him.

He felt that the grenade in Rachmat's trouser pocket was attracting the attention of everyone in the restaurant. Rachmat's face was tense, and even in Hazil there was a change. He spoke more quickly than usual, and there was something forced in his calm movements.

His speech could not conceal his tenseness. A cold sweat soaked Isa's chest, stomach, and the whole length of his spine. He wanted to scream, weep, yell and run, run run. But he didn't run. He didn't scream. He didn't cry. He didn't yell. He sat there drinking his glass of fruit juice, unconscious of the bitter sweetness of the drink, continually asking himself how he had got there. Why was he with them? Those two youths were carrying grenades in their trousers' pockets. And even worse, he realised now what was going to happen next. He could see it in his mind's eye. They were going to throw the grenades and then run; to throw the grenades into the midst of the Dutch soldiers crowding out of the cinema.

He still remembered how Hazil had come one afternoon to his house—was it a day ago, two, three days ago—a week, a month, a year, ten years? Isa could no longer remember, nor could he count—so distant were the days not concerned with the grenade throwing, not concerned with him sitting in the restaurant waiting for the exodus from the cinema.

It seemed another person who had opened the door to Hazil that afternoon—a stranger who lived in another world—not him—because he could not be so mad as to carry a hand-grenade to hurl it into the midst of the crowd when the cinema came out.

'I'm not one for violence,' he had whispered that afternoon when Hazil had outlined the plan ordered by Headquarters outside the city. There were always orders coming from out of town. The spirit of people in Djakarta was growing feeble, they were losing confidence that the struggle for Freedom would end in victory. That was how the letter had begun. A letter he had neither read nor seen. It was only Hazil who had told them there was such a letter, and that their group had been ordered to begin underground operations against the Dutch. It had to prove to the people that the struggle for Freedom continued everywhere. The outside world had to be given proof that even in Djakarta, totally under Dutch military control, the warriors of the Republic could harry the enemy. 'I'm not one for violence,' he whispered again; and Hazil looked at him and said simply, 'Neither am I. I am a composer.'

That answer made it even more difficult for him to say anything—to demur or to object. He saw no point in hurling the grenade. It was a useless act. If Hazil had been annoyed and shouted at him, perhaps he would have been obstinate, and dared to reject the suggestion.

He felt he was in a world gone mad; or was it he who was mad? It was no longer possible to tell the difference. Was he or the world mad, or Hazil, or the plan or the Headquarters outside the city? It was as though he were in a dark, impenetrable forest, in every direction his way was blocked and there was nothing for him but to take the line of least resistance. Then Hazil told him he and Rachmat were to throw the grenades and that Isa had to be there only to see whether they were successful or arrested or shot, and to report the outcome of their plan. If they were successful, Isa was to go straight home and wait until one of them came to him. If, within two days, he had no news this meant they had been arrested, and he was to report this to the Headquarters at Krawang.

Then Isa was no longer capable of refusing—rather, beside his fear there arose a feeling of embarrassment, and fear for the safety of Hazil and Rachmat. They had chosen the most dangerous part of the job, and he had only to watch. He merely said that he would do it, and Hazil shook his hand and behaved as though he had decided to sacrifice his life on an important mission. And Hazil had said, 'Just think. We appear in public, eat and sleep, and say we belong to the underground; but what do we do? We are terrified and hide if a precinct is searched. Our hearts tremble at the mere sight of the Dutch military police. We speak of the Revolution; but what do we do?' Isa did not answer. What could he say?

Fortunately, there had only been two nights between Hazil's visit and this evening. But during those two nights, his terror-filled dreams swept over him again and again, pounding him like a tempestuous sea, the rolling waves surging over him, taking him into their depths, hurling him out, choking him; and again and again he awoke panting, soaked in a cold sweat.

The following morning, a bitter taste clung to his mouth, far worse than usual. He felt weak and an urge to vomit compressed his stomach.

Fatima was not told where they were going that evening. This was Hazil's suggestion. Isa had a strange feeling towards Fatima now. They had grown so far apart that sometimes when he awoke from the terror of his nightmares and saw Fatima beautiful and untroubled asleep beside him, he felt he was lying next to a stranger—a woman he did not know.

He knew that he could not come to Fatima with his loneliness. He could not come to her with his fear, his terror, his sorrows, or his joys. Moments of joy rarely came to him now. If indeed he was finding his way out of the forest, and the trees were thinning out, it was only to come to a hard, dry desert.

Since he had found Hazil's pipe under the pillow, whether it was yesterday or a century ago, it was as if something had died within his heart—something fresh which no matter how black his terror, had always been there. Now it was gone. But he was still too frightened to admit that it was gone, and still hoped against hope that it was not; so he kept the pipe hidden in his desk drawer.

He was afraid that if he made an issue of the pipe everything he had feared all this time would be confirmed. And this he wanted to avoid. He was aware that everything was over between Fatima and himself, but he wanted to postpone his admission of it as long as he could.

A woman went along the road, passing close to their table at the edge of the restaurant. Isa saw her look at them and smile, but it meant nothing to him. He heard, but he did not understand, Rachmat saying as he nudged Hazil:

'How about her, Hazil? Look at the swing of her hips.'

'O, you're crazy—any woman and you're drooling at the mouth.' Rachmat laughed, quickly checked himself and looked at the bottom of his glass. The light of the lamp played on it and the remnants of the beer with the little bubbles of froth, reminded Hazil of something, the froth on the mouth of the irregular who had been shot, near Klender. Only, the froth on his mouth had been flecked red with blood. Rachmat shook his head.

'Now!' said Hazil, and Rachmat and Isa were roused from their thoughts. Crowds were beginning to come out from the cinema.

The three of them got up. Each knew what he had to do. Hazil went to pay for their drinks and then vanished in the crowd. Rachmat followed him and took up a position by a small kiosk. Isa stood outside the restaurant.

He waited. He had to wait there until he heard two grenade explosions and to check whether Hazil or Rachmat came to any harm. Then he had to hurry home.

As he stood at the side of the road by the restaurant, time as it flowed over him seemed to pass very slowly. In front of the cinema, dense crowds of people on their way home were jostling against each other like water bursting out of an opened channel. The sound of the pedicab bells and the cries of their drivers looking for fares blended with the horns of the cars whose chauffeurs were impatiently waiting. A number one tram came and stopped, and the crowds surged together, struggling to get on.

Now, thought Isa, now. Now. Now. But there was still no explosion. He was still afraid, but there was another feeling in his heart now—a feeling of superiority to the masses of people crowded together like a herd of cattle in front of the cinema. He knew what was going to happen a moment later and they did not. As this sensation blended with that of fear, he felt his head light like a balloon about to float up into the air.

Isa did not know when the first grenade went off. The explosion startled him, even though he had been so long expecting it. It wasn't until the second grenade exploded that Isa realised that Rachmat and Hazil had done their part.

Now it was his turn, but he did not know what to do.

The two grenade explosions in quick succession created an immense confusion. It was as though the stroke of a huge invisible fan had swept over the crowd in front of the cinema milling through Senen Square. There were screams and shouts and people running in all directions. Some soldiers fired a few rounds, others responded. The rattle of sten and rifle fire blended with the cries of pain and panic.

In a moment, the area in front of the cinema and Senen Square was deserted. A few pedicabs remained; an overturned tin of peanuts scattered around—the table and the pan of the fried banana seller, the fire in the charcoal stoves still glowing, the shops hastily shut and the lamps extinguished.

The sound of the firing died away. But the silence of the square was soon split by the screams of sirens on the jeeps of the Dutch Military Police. Their white-painted steel helmets were like skulls in the darkness of the night.

Quickly and systematically they surrounded the Square and began to investigate. Two soldiers lying in front of the cinema entrance were quickly taken away into an ambulance. Several others moaning because of wounds were picked up and given first aid. A few Military Police with torches were looking for fragments of the grenades.

Isa panicked when the second grenade went off. He forgot he had to wait to see what happened. Quickly he hurled himself into the masses of people running to escape.

He stopped running when he was out of breath, and he staggered, gasping, his chest splitting; the stream of people running had thinned out, and he came to a stop by a gate in a fence in a small side street. He was very frightened.

After he had stood leaning there for a few minutes the door of the house opened and a man looked out. Isa was on the point of asking for shelter, but as soon as the man saw him he shut the door again quickly.

When he saw the door close, Isa's terror multiplied. He knew perfectly well what had happened, what Rachmat and Hazil had done, and his association with the two of them. The fear of the man who had hastily shut the door, increased his own fear.

I must get home he whispered to himself, trying to control the thudding of his heart and sharpness piercing his chest; but it beat all the harder. I must get home— quickly, quickly, he whispered.

He moved on but at the end of the alley he stopped. The Kwitang thoroughfare was dark, empty and silent. From where he stood he could see an army truck and Military Police jeep standing in the middle of the road near the number 1 tram stop. He left the alley and hurried quickly towards the Kebon Sireh intersection. He had only taken a few steps when he heard the sound of a fast driven jeep behind him. He dodged behind a tree, and when the jeep head-lights reached the place where he had been standing, Isa was no longer there. He leant against the tree, panting again and his heart thudding.

The jeep sped on across the bridge and disappeared round the bend of the Kebon Sireh intersection. He set off again walking quickly, his heart thudding. This was the climax of his terror alone along a dark, silent, deserted road. He felt he was walking to the scaffold, stark naked in broad daylight, watched by his pupils.

I don't want to have anything more to do with it, he thought to himself. 'I don't want anything more to do with it,' he said. 'Never again, never again,' he repeated. 'I don't want to—don't want to, not any more, never again.'

After this, I only want to live, he said to himself, I only want to stay alive. I don't want to be involved either with the Republic, or with the Dutch. I just want to be a teacher and stay alive—just that.

He thought back to the days of Dutch rule. As far as he was concerned, it was a much better time than the present, he said to himself. Then a person could work and live in peace. Even the Japanese occupation was better than this even with the menace of the Kenpeitai* lurking in the background. But now life and work was impossible.

He was scared to death when suddenly his name was called. 'Isa! Isa!'—a voice both urgent and carrying authority. His first instinct was to flee. But when he heard the voice go on, 'It's us here, Hazil and Rachmat,' a hot and cold feeling of relief flowed over him, filling all the cavities in his body until for a moment he almost forgot the fear that was throttling him. He broke into a trot, leapt over a monsoon drain and stepped behind a stone house wall.

Hazil and Rachmat were crouching there, close together. Hazil seized his shoulder telling him to crouch beside them.

'You were walking alone, a picture of guilt,' Hazil said to him. 'If I were a Dutch soldier you would be the first person I would arrest. It was obvious you were trying to escape.'

*Japanese Secret Police.

'How did we do?' asked Rachmat. Isa felt again the immensity of his fear.

'I saw two men sprawled on the ground—they were taken away by ambulance,' he said, anxious to be rid of the story, 'and there were many wounded.'

'Hell—only two', cursed Rachmat. The three of them remained silent for a few moments until Rachmat said, 'Let's go home now. We'd better separate.'

'I'll take Isa home,' said Hazil, realising Isa's fear.

Rachmat got up, leapt out over the fence, and hurried into the shadow of some trees and vanished into Gang Nangka. Isa watched him go and felt it was his own body vanishing with him.

'It's our turn' said Hazil. 'Just walk naturally even if a jeep or anything passes by. If we run from its headlights, they'll chase us.' The pair of them stood up and walked out.

Although still frightened, Isa felt somewhat calmer now. Hazil was silent and Isa had no inclination to speak. He was incapable of speech after the experience of that night.

9

After Hazil had gone on to his house and the servant girl had opened the door to him, Isa felt very strange. His house seemed new and unfamiliar to him, as though there were something he did not recognise. So far had his feelings changed, or he had changed as a result of his feelings after arriving indoors from the street full of menace. Fatima was asleep, or was pretending to be asleep. I could have been killed tonight and it wouldn't mean anything to her, thought Isa, bitterly. And unjustly, because Fatima had not known their plans. Fatima's slumber only increased his sense of the gulf between them. That night he slept alone although beside Fatima in the dark room, in the close embrace of his fears.

The wind rustling in the nangka trees to him took on the sound of the Military Police whispering together, as they planned to swoop on his house, and the snap of an old branch dropping onto the roof, became in his mind a savage knock on the door. This impression was so vivid on one occasion that Isa leapt up out of bed, ran to the back door of the bedroom and hid in the space between the wall and the cupboard. His body trembled, his knees shook, his breathing laboured, his heart went cold in the clasp of fear. For a few moments he stood half-crouching, like a wild animal trapped, unable to flee. Fear swept over him like the waves of the sea crashing onto the shore battering him. The fear surging around him that night was not just his own, but that of all humanity; all the fear man had known fell upon him in that one moment, throttling him in the corner between the wall and the cupboard: little Salim's, Fatima's, his own fear; the fears of Hazil, of Saleh who evacuated, of Hamidy, of all who could not sleep that night, who slept restlessly, who dreamt in leaky hovels, in houses, palaces, villages, cities, valleys, mountains, at sea, in the air—wherever in the world there were human creatures: the fear of all the soldiers of every battlefield from the dawn of history until now; the fear of Christians hurled by Nero to the lions at Rome, the fear of primitive man of gods and demons, the fear of wild animals of their hunters, the fear of the deer in the coils of the snake, all these fears came upon him at once, crushing, pounding, pressing, battering him in that narrow space between the wall and the cup-board, all these and still more.

There Isa stood half-crouching, his eyes wild, his breathing laboured and his chest aching—his knees shaking and his stomach cold and empty. Surging waves of human fear from every corner of the globe came pounding upon him, carried by the tide of time sweeping unceasingly past him. How long was he there? Seconds passed like centuries creeping slowly by.

Then he realised that the whispering he had heard was only the rustling of the wind in the nangka leaves. The liberation he felt was as though the demon of fear clasping him in a sexual embrace had discharged its semen, and left him weak and trembling. He would have fallen without the cupboard to support him, as he waited for his heart beat to calm, and the throbbing in the pit of his stomach to ease. A cold sweat drenched the nape of his neck and his back. Then he looked at the bed. Fatima was still sleeping soundly. And at the sight of her Isa felt a momentary jealously tinged with hatred. But this feeling too subsided just as had the waves of fear.

Isa could not sleeep soundly after that. He tossed restlessly, continually disturbed by the weight of anxiety and **fear.** Just before dawn, he was awakened **again by** the sound of little Salim crying in the next room. Isa got up and went to him.

Salim lay there sobbing but when Isa came **in he** checked his tears and pretended to be asleep. Isa bent over him, took his shoulder and said. 'Salim, why are you crying? Did you have a nightmare?' His own voice trembled a little though he didn't realise it.

Salim still pretended to be asleep, and Isa repeated the question. Slowly Salim opened his eyes and looked at Isa.

'I'm frightened,' he said softly. The word 'frightened' uttered by the little child struck Isa like a heavy blow. For a few moments there was nothing he could say or do, he stood bent over looking at Salim. And Salim became afraid to look at him, and his lip trembled, as though he were about to cry again; then Isa came to his senses. He quickly sat on the bed and stroked Salim's head.

'Afraid. What are you afraid of? he asked gently.

'I'm afraid to sleep alone in the dark,' the child answered.

Isa understood what he meant. He realised that Salim had slept alone for years like this; every night had been filled with fear, and he had lived alone with his fear. He knew the feeling, but he didn't know what to say.

'If I put on the light will you still be afraid?' he asked.

Salim shook his head.

Isa got up and switched on the light. 'There you are,' he said. 'It's light now. There's nothing to be afraid of. Go to sleep'.

Salim smiled at him gratefully and Isa went back to his room. He carefully lowered himself onto the bed but lay awake till dawn. All manner of thoughts disturbed him and when he fell asleep the sky was bright. He woke as Fatima opened the window, his mouth was sour and his breath foul. He had forgotten to put his denture in a glass.

That day at school, Isa felt ill. Everyone was talking about the hand-grenade throwing in front of the Rex Cinema, and although he felt a satisfaction to hear the pupils and the teachers praise the grenade-throwers, Isa still felt oppressed with fear that at any moment the Military Police would come to the school and arrest him.

While he was teaching and during the recess, Isa often thought of little Salim, feeling somewhat embarrassed and contemptuous of himself. Isa saw how alike they were—both full of fear—even though they were not afraid of the same things. But the emotion of fear in both was the same. Perhaps Salim's fear was even greater than that which he felt. And Salim had borne this fear for years. To look at him you would not realise that he had lived with fear for so long. He still played like other children, sang like other children, but the fear he suffered last night . . . Isa's thoughts stopped as he remembered his own fear. He felt surprised to think that a little child like Salim could know fear. Then gradually he began to realise that one must accept and live with fear. He had to follow the example of little Salim. How can it be done? he asked himself. Must everyone live with his own fear? Must he learn to live with his fear? Or can fear be cast aside? Does everyone have his own fear—or are there some who never know fear at any time or in any circumstances?

As he took the last hour, his thoughts were not on the lesson. He looked at the pupils and asked himself what fears they had to live with. He thought of his colleagues, and other teachers. They, too, had their own fears. And Fatima—what did she fear? And Hazil and Rachmat, and Hazil's father—everyone.

He wanted the class quickly over. He wanted to go home to be with little Salim again.

10

When the news came it was unexpected. It broke like a thunderbolt. Isa was reading the paper at the stall at Gang Djaksa. It was just a week since the grenade-throwing; and during that week neither Hazil nor Rachmat had come to his house. This was not surprising because they had already told him that after that night it might be a long time before they came. He was beginning to learn to live with his fear. Even though his fear still disturbed him, now he was learning to control the racing of his heart when the waves of fear pounded upon it. During the week, nothing had happened and he was beginning to feel calm again.

No longer, while teaching, eating, bathing, or in the privy, was he expecting a brutal arrest by the Military Police.

So the news headline struck him like a thunderbolt.

GRENADE THROWER ARRESTED!

The headline was followed by a report that, thanks to the thoroughness and skill of the Police, one of the grenade-throwers in front of the Rex Cinema the previous week, had been arrested. His name was not mentioned, but it was stated that he had admitted he was involved, and that the Police were proceeding with their enquiries.

Isa stiffened and went cold; panic seized him. His heart throbbed painfully. He sat stock-still, his eyes fixed on the newspaper, oblivious of anything else. The letters blurred, twisted, and spun in disorder. The white newsprint turned pitch black.

He fainted and the newspaper dropped from his hand as he sprawled back in the chair. The store owner and the few people drinking coffee were startled. 'The teacher's fainted' one of them exclaimed.

The owner got a glass of cold water, dipped his fingers into it and stroked them across Isa's forehead. Someone else undid his shirt collar and they lifted him carefully on to a bench.

A few moments later, Isa opened his eyes.

'Ah! He's coming to,' said someone.

They stood around looking at him. Gradually the blackness dispersed and Isa saw first the waists of the people who were standing around the bench, then their chests, then their necks and then their faces, as they looked at him with anxiety and relief.

Isa felt embarrassed and his fear swiftly returned. But he was able to say 'I'm sorry. I've not been feeling well today,' and he tried to get up. The bystanders helped him and eventually he stood up and leaned on the back of a chair. 'It's all right now', he said. 'I can go home myself.'

They watched him leave the stall and start walking slowly homeward.

But there was a tempest in his heart. Who had been arrested—Rachmat or Hazil? Why hadn't they given him any news? Would the one arrested keep his mouth shut? Had he told everything? I'm going to be arrested . . . I'm going to be arrested. I must run—run. Don't go home. The Police are waiting there. Go—run—right now. But where? Where can I run? Hide in the house of a friend. Who would dare hide me?

When he got home he saw little Salim playing in the yard. He went indoors and without saying anything, went into his study and shut the door.

When Fatima knocked at eight o'clock, Isa did not answer. And when she came in and asked him if he wanted anything to eat, he replied that he had no appetite and pretended to be engrossed in a book. After she had gone out again, closing the door behind her, Isa stayed alone with his fear in the little room.

The sound of footsteps passing through the alley in front of the house was like a tramp of the feet of Military Police coming to arrest him. A feverish shivering seized him and he felt cold and scared.

Not until far into the night, when he knew that Fatima was asleep, did he get up from his chair and throw himself onto the bed.

When he woke the next morning, his mouth was sour. He had again forgotten to take out his denture. And he didn't get out of bed. He felt ill. The whole morning he was expecting the Military Police to come to arrest him, the pressure of his fear grew progressively greater.

Then night returned and now Isa was ill, with a very

high fever. Fatima moved to sleep with little Salim, and Isa stayed alone in the room with his fever, with his fear and the terrifying nameless shadows. The sound of the leaves rustling in the wind—the crack of a dry branch, the secret sounds of the night blended with his fears and the phantasms of his fever.

Morning came without bringing the Military Police to arrest him. Two days and two nights, Isa lay ill, every moment expecting the Police while the phantasms of his fever danced like demons about his room. But still the Police did not come.

It was three days before Isa dared to get out of bed and to sit on the steps of the front of the house. The fear, like a disease, flogging his body, had begun to subside.

It was then that the Police came. A Military Policeman, followed by two civilians. They came in, pushing open the squeaky bamboo gate, and suddenly they were standing in front of him. One of the civilians said to him respectfully.

'We are looking for Isa, the school teacher. Is that you?'

Isa felt his fear return, but not with the violence he had imagined. It was a strange feeling. He was afraid, but did not panic.

'I am Isa,' he replied.

The man in civilian clothes who first spoke continued respectfully. 'I'm afraid we have instructions to take you to headquarters.'

It was only then that he realised he was being arrested. His heart thudded, the pain throbbed and for a moment he stumbled as though about to fall. But he pulled himself together and said, 'Very well.' His voice trembled.

He stood up.

'You'd better take a few clothes,' the man said. Isa got up and went inside. The three of them followed him. Fatima was in the back room and, hearing the tramp of footsteps, came out. She went pale at the sight of the Military Police. 'What is it?' she exclaimed in alarm.

'They are taking me to the Police Station,' said Isa. 'Get a few things ready.'

Fatima ran into the room bewildered. Now it was Isa who was calm. The fear I had imagined was greater than the reality, he thought. He was still very frightened but could control the fear.

He went into the bedroom followed by the man who had first spoken to him. He put into his case a vest, a sarong, underpants and two shirts.

'Give me a cake of soap,' he said to Fatima. His voice trembled. He knew that the only cake of soap they had was in the bathroom.

Fatima went to the bathroom swaying slightly, still unable to grasp the full import of what was happening. Isa put the soap in his bag then said in a somewhat hoarse and trembling voice.

'I am ready.'

He looked at Fatima and said, 'Take good care of Salim and the house,' then quickly turned round and walked out of the room. As he reached the front verandah he heard Fatima crying, and he asked himself whether she wept because she loved him or because of the thought of the difficulties which would face her when he was gone.

He felt fear mixed with bitterness.

They walked to the main road. The neighbours looked at Isa amid the three men. They said nothing and Isa felt their eyes following him. At the main road a jeep driven by another Military Policeman was waiting. Isa's legs were weak and trembling when they told him to get in and to sit at the back, but he managed it. The Military Policeman with the pistol sat beside him. One civilian sat in front of him, and the other man who had first addressed him sat beside the driver. The driver started the engine and the jeep moved off.

It was only then that Isa saw a few yards behind him another jeep, and a group of men from it were going into the alley.

They're going to search the house, he thought. The jeep sped away from Gang Djaksa past the houses and stalls, telephone poles, people, children he had seen every day—clearly and sharply defined like pictures in a black frame.

At Djalan Kebon Sireh the Military Policeman beside him took out a pack of cigarettes and after putting one into his own mouth, offered one to Isa. The action gave a feeling of relief to Isa who was choked with fear. He thanked him in a trembling voice and put the cigarette in his mouth. The Military Policeman lit his own cigarette and offered the light to Isa. In his haste to accept the light and to please the Military Policeman, Isa put out the cigarette lighter. The policeman lit it again. Isa's fear returned, fear that the Military Policeman would be irritated and angry with him—but he lit the lighter again and proffered it to Isa a third time. At last Isa was successful and an extraordinary feeling of relief rose in his breast. But it did not last long. The fragrance of the tobacco, the pleasure of smoking, soon lost its savour. He thought of what awaited him. He thought of Fatima. Of Salim. He wondered who had been captured, Rachmat or Hazil? Who had confessed? He thought of Hazil's pipe he had found under the pillow still hidden in his desk drawer. He was afraid that the police now searching his house would open the drawer and Fatima would see the pipe and realise that he had found it. Then he thought of his childhood, of the new suit he got at Lebaran; how his father beat him because he had broken a jar filled with sweetmeats; he remembered his first bicycle, a present from his father when he was promoted to the sixth grade. He thought of his first attempt to make love when he was at the Teacher's Training College. He thought of Tien. He thought of all kinds of other things. He thought of his fear and felt such terror that he could think of nothing else, only fear. And his fear increased in magnitude until he began to temble.

He was taken to a small room in the Military Police Barracks at Laan Trivelli. It was empty. He was alone. No table. No chair. No divan. No mat. The window was barred. It was an average size window. There were only four bars. From behind them he could see the deep blue sky and fleecy white clouds. But for the bars it would have been like any other small room. And his fear. He heard the sound of a door slammed to, the sound of a key; he was on his own.

His loneliness in the room opened up all the dammed up channels of his fear. It poured out foaming with a roar. Isa panicked. He felt like a mouse caught in a trap: the room was the trap and he was the mouse.

At that moment the primitive fear of man came to a peak and ran wild in the room.

But two hours later when the door opened again and he was taken to the investigation room, the climax of his fear was past. Now, just as at the time of his arrest at his house, the fear that he had imagined was much worse than the reality.

He was taken to a room in the middle of the Barracks. Two stern-faced Military Policemen stood at the door. He went in staggering and feeble, his heart thudding against his breast.

In the room there was a rough table and behind it a man in uniform with the insignia of a Captain on his shoulders. A drawn pistol lay on the table—a few heaps of papers, a bottle of ink and two pens black with ink. Behind him stood another Military Policeman, and in front of the table a rickety chair.

He was ordered to be seated, and with a heart filled with dread, he sat and waited.

The Captain raised his head. He was still young but his face was cruel and his mouth was a thin, level line. His nose was swollen from a boxing injury; he looked strong. When Isa was seated the Captain looked him in the face sharply, and Isa's heart beat even faster.

'Are you Isa?' he asked. His voice was coarse and staccato.

'Yes, Sir. I am Isa,' he replied with a tremor in his voice. Something like a smile formed on the thin line of the Captain's mouth. It pleased him to hear that tremor.

'Do you know why you've been arrested?' he then asked.

Isa was bewildered. He knew perfectly well why he had been arrested. But if he admitted this, did it not mean he would have to tell everything and betray Hazil and Rachmat and all of them? He was uncertain and the Captain saw his uncertainty.

'We know everything,' he said in warning, his voice

sharp and menacing. 'You had better confess. Your arrested colleague has told us everything.'

Isa grew more frightened and uncertain. He was afraid that if he did not confess he would be tortured and forced to talk. But if he confessed, and what the Captain said was not true, then he would be a traitor. He was afraid to confess and equally afraid of being a traitor.

He looked hopelessly at the Captain. His tongue was stiff and he could not utter a word. In his chest it was as if a large drum were beaten loudly, Boom, Boom, Boom, the longer, the louder; then everything went black and Isa fainted.

When he came to, he was in another room. He was lying on the floor and when he opened his eyes the first thing he saw was the barred window. The sky was still very blue and the clouds very white. Then he realised that there was someone else in the room. For a moment he lay still and closed his eyes again. Then he tried to sit up. He felt two hands help him raise his shoulders and he was startled to hear Hazil's voice:

'Isa, it's me.'

He scarcely recognised the voice. He leant against the wall and slowly turned his head.

'Hazil,' he said. There was almost a joy in his voice; but the words which were to follow were cut short when he saw Hazil. His lips were split; two of his upper front teeth were missing. A deep gash was drying on his forehead, his face was pale and thin, and his eyes bloodshot.

Isa was startled and for a long time speechless. He just stared at Hazil. Did they torture you? he said to himself in terror.

Hazil lowered his eyes to avoid Isa's glance. I betrayed him. I betrayed him, he accused himself. Now he is here facing the same torment as myself because I was a coward and could not stand torture. Hazil lowered his head to his chest, filled with the disgrace to his manhood, ashamed before the friend he had betrayed. And he sobbed like a little child.

Isa continued to look at him. Gradually, very gradually, he understood what Hazil was saying through his sobs, 'I have done wrong. I have been disloyal. I could not stand their torture—could not stand their torture. Let me die now. Let me redeem my treachery. Let me die—forgive me—forgive me'. And seeing Hazil like this—Hazil who had been a true warrior, courageous and full of spirit after only a week in their custody, beaten into a creature to be pitied, weeping, begging forgiveness, a strange feeling arose in Isa's heart.

The dark strength which could destroy a man like Hazil was an evil strength, a strength to be fought and conquered. But he felt himself too small and too full of fear to be able to fight and to conquer it.

Then the door was opened and the Captain who had interrogated him earlier entered, followed by two Military Policemen.

'You are conscious again,' he said. His voice had not changed, tense, harsh and cold.

'Have you had a chance to talk?' he asked.

Isa looked at Hazil sinking into himself, shrinking away from them.

'He's confessed everything,' said the Captain. 'It was he who threw the grenade with another called Rachmat; and you have charge of the funds for the irregulars in the city. Where is Rachmat hiding? Where are the funds hidden? Who else are republican irregulars in the city?' His voice became harsh and heavy with menace.

Isa was terrified. The young Captain stood near the door. One of the Military Policemen approached Isa and barked at him: 'Answer! Tell us.'

Isa became more terrified—his tongue went stiff. His heart ordered him to speak and confess, to confess as quickly as possible before he was tortured like Hazil. His whole being cried out to him: 'Tell them at once.' But when he opened his mouth to speak, there was no sound. He was too frightened. Suddenly he had wet his pants.

'Get up!' shouted the Military Policeman to him. His whole being cried out to him to get up. But he could not stand. Like a fool, not like himself, he looked at the floor—a filthy, dusty floor; then into his circle of vision came the toe of a great boot—then another. Isa stiffened into immobility. He groaned quietly in his fear. He saw the boot rise slowly and disappear from his circle of vision. Then he suddenly felt something huge and heavy crash onto his chest. It was as though his breath were hurled out of the cavity of his lungs and his ribs were crushed. His heart cried in anguish and when the second kick came Isa could hear only the sound of a heavily beating drum which faded into the distance and lost its definition; he felt himself drifting, swallowed up in darkness.

Hazil watched, trembling, while the soldier went on kicking Isa lying sprawled on the floor. Then the young Captain said something and the soldier stopped. They left the room and locked the door, leaving Hazil pale and trembling twisting his hands.

For a while time ceased to flow for the pair of them in

that little room, then Isa opened his eyes and groaned. Hazil went to him and tried to help him sit up; but Isa resisted his hand, said hoarsely in a broken voice, 'Never mind,' and then, 'My denture.' Hazil picked up the plate which had fallen onto the floor and gave it to him.

He lay there, his eyes looking out of the window. The sky was still very blue and the clusters of clouds very white. Hazil said to him.

'Isa, tell them. They'll come back.'

Isa was still unable to speak, and his chest hurt terribly. 'They'll come back. They'll come back.' The words went like a refrain through his head. 'They'll come back. They'll come back, they'll come back'—full of menace and fear.

And they came back. But every time Isa wanted to confess, he went speechless with fear and the rain of blows made him incapable of speech.

They came back. During the night—the following day, that night—the following day—the next night—until it was impossible to keep any track of time; outside the sky grew more blue and the clouds more white. Alternately Isa and Hazil were kicked and beaten and Isa saw Hazil gradually disintegrate as a man and as a human being. The fear of torture and the pain constantly increased their hold over him until fear ruled his personality.

Hazil told everything. A slap on the face sufficed to make him speak.

In the room, time had ceased to flow and Isa felt a change within himself. Physical pain no longer scared him. He knew he would be tortured at fixed intervals and there was no change in the pain he felt. But a strange feeling insinuated itself into his heart; because he no longer felt afraid of a beating or torture—his yearning to confess also disappeared.

And gradually, without realising it, he began to feel pity at the sight of Hazil; and together with the feeling of pity there arose a hatred for the dark strength that could destroy a man like Hazil.

During the times they were alone together, he tried to speak to him. 'I'm not angry with you—I don't hate you,' he said. 'What you did, I wanted to do, and in my mind I have done long ago; but every time I wanted to confess, the blows and the kicks made it impossible to speak. My whole being urged me to confess, but my tongue was tied with pain and fear. But we must not yield now. One must learn to live with fear'. Isa stopped for a moment. Now everything was clear to him, as though a streak of lightning had illumined his heart. Now he understood. Everyone lives with and tries to hide fear. A rich man fears the loss of his property, the leader fears he will be outmanoeuvred. Salim feared devils and ghosts. Everyone has his own fear and must learn to live with and conquer it.

Even they, the harsh soldiers who tortured him were full of fear. The greater their fear, the more cruel they were. But I don't know how I can explain this to Hazil, he thought.

Then he thought of recalling to Hazil, Hazil's own words; but he did not utter them, because everything that Hazil had said before stood in judgment on Hazil now. Words such as, 'I am bound by the trust and loyalty of my friends. Is music more important than loyalty to a friend?' Isa recalled Hazil's words: 'This music sings a struggle of mankind as man. Mankind as individuals. Do you know what I mean? How can I explain it? The struggle of mankind, not as a herd, not the bark of jackals hunting in a pack, but the bark and growl in the grief and the cry of the individual jackal struggling for life. For me the individual is an end and not the means to achieve an end. Human happiness consists of the perfect harmony of the individual with other human beings. The State is only a means. And the individual must not be subordinated to the State. This is the music of my life. This is my struggle. This is the road I follow—the road with no end. This is the Revolution which we have begun. Revolution is only the means to achieve freedom and freedom itself is only a means—a means to enrich the happiness and the nobility of human life'.

Then Isa realised that now all this was meaningless to Hazil and he felt grieved for him. Hazil who was young, who sat leaning against the wall in the corner, speechless, his eyes dim, hollow-cheeked, and pale.

And suddenly, Isa realised that Hazil would die and felt a deep grief.

But at the same time, he realised that a new road was open for himself. All that Hazil had said before, which he now remembered in that room, was for him. He had gained mastery of himself. It was not that he no longer felt fear, but he had made peace with his fear. He had learnt how to live with it.

When, one morning Isa awoke, whenever it was, because time had no meaning in that room where Time had ceased to flow, he felt the blood course hot and vigorous through his veins—throughout all his sinews and he realised he was happy. His virility had returned—he wished to leap, to cry out, to proclaim his happiness to the whole world. Outside, the sky grew ever more blue and the clouds ever more white. He stood in front of the window, holding the bars in his two hands, and time began to flow again for him—to flow onwards, filled with the fire of life.

In the corner of the room, Hazil lay groaning, pursued by dreams of terror.

And when Isa heard again the tramp of footsteps approaching their cell, he felt at peace with the fear within him. He knew that their terror could no longer touch him. He was free.